Ba
T.

To "off" deserving senior males
Whose lives are weighed and judged as "fails."
The story, picaresque at first,
May make you laugh until you burst;
But then you find its theme depends
On growing old with best of friends.
Evoking laughter, thoughtful tears,
It tells the story of our years."
— Lee Johnson, author of *Poetria Nova*

The Toby Martin Pet Detective Series

"I HAVE GROWN up reading and writing reviews for these humorous books about the mystery solving sleuth, Toby Martin. As Toby's character has grown over the years I too, have grown with her. Sharing in many similarities, especially the curly hair. This was such a heartfelt way to end the "Toby Martin: Pet Detective" Era. We say farewell to Toby but we will always cherish the feisty playfulness she brought to this extraordinary series, written by an even more extraordinary woman."
— Ellie Capistrant, 16, a student at Roseville Area High School, Roseville, MN

"THIS BOOK IS FANTASTIC! I could not stop reading it and was told off by my mom for still being up at two in the morning. Also I read it three times and I am still reading the book. To put it together in one sentence: it was impossible to put down."
— Alice Dobson, age 11, Düsseldorf, Germany

"A GIRL HARRY POTTER! Toby is spunky and Mrs. Trattles is snake-like. A great fun read!"
— Caleb Twiggs, age 12, Roseville, Minnesota

For Lee,
my "rainbow connection —
the lovers, the dreamers,
and Lee"
xo Barbara
Happy 5th!

The Rainbow House

by Barbara Grengs

Cambridge Books
an imprint of
WriteWords, Inc.
CAMBRIDGE, MD 21613

𝕮𝖆𝖒𝖇𝖗𝖎𝖉𝖌𝖊 𝕭𝖔𝖔𝖐𝖘 is a subsidiary of:

Write Words, Inc.
2934 Old Route 50
Cambridge, MD 21613

ISBN 978-1-61386-426-5

Fax: 410-221-7510

Bowker Standard Address Number: 254-0304

DEDICATION

For Gabe
(December 2006-April 2018)
More Gentleman than Border Collie

Author's Note

I am not a farmer. I have never met runty pigs. I'm ignorant about chickens and goat care. Therefore, any inaccuracies or inconsistencies are the fault of the animals. Please forgive them.

But I did teach in Hastings 1966-67, live outside of Hastings on 210th Street E. from 1996-98, go to King's regularly, shop at the Village General Antiques store, and visit Sylvia's gardens almost daily. I saw and experienced the best of the area and wanted to celebrate both Hastings and Miesville in *The Rainbow House.*

The Rainbow House

The flock of bluebirds on the birthday card started it. The color of the summer sky on their backs, the color of rusty metal on their breasts. I can still hear my mother warning me about rusty nails and blood poisoning, giving statistics to prove her point.

As the optimist in the family, Carrie, my kid sister, thought the bluebirds were a sign of happy things to come. At age sixteen, when I thought I was worldly and mature, I dismissed such superstitions as childish. Now at age seventy I'm inclined to embrace Carrie's perspective.

The birthday card was from Aunt Maggie who invited Carrie and me to spend the summer with her in Miesville, Minnesota where the Miesville Mudhens were the small town version of the New York Yankees, and King's Bar served the best 'burgers and fries in Minnesota.

Whoever heard of Miesville anyway? At the time I didn't appreciate her gift. Now I do.

I'm Suzan Bailey Stoddard and I remember that magical summer as though it happened yesterday.

> *"We had the experience but missed the meaning."*
>
> *—T.S. Eliot*

CHAPTER 1

The Invite

June, 1964

Even though I didn't want to spend my summer with zany earth mother Aunt Maggie, Carrie and I needed to escape Mom and Dad's drama. Every day was a crisis: Move or not? New jobs or not? Stay married or not? The arguing was wearing us down, especially now that we didn't have school as a distraction.

"Girls, you've got a card from Aunt Maggie," Mom yelled from the kitchen, as she was going through the mail and drinking her morning tea. Carrie, my dopey eight-year-old sister, burst into the kitchen like it was Christmas morning and not just a dumb card.

Let me explain about Aunt Maggie, mom's younger sister. Other than sharing the same parents, they had nothing in common.

Mom looked like all the other moms in our neighborhood: mostly permed short hair which they had "done" at the Beauty School to save money. They never wore shorts, pedal pushers, or pants because that would be immodest. Instead they wore at or below-the-knee shirtwaist print dresses or skirts, blouses and nylons with sensible flats, usually black. When they went downtown to pay the bills, they dressed up which meant they put on a dab of makeup and a hat that matched their outfits. Maybe they changed into low-heeled pumps or accessorized with gloves. I thought they looked tired, old and frumpy.

Add blah and boring to tired, old and frumpy and you'd describe our house. We lived just a few blocks from the St. Cloud hospital in a tan three-bedroom rambler aside other three bedroom ramblers painted various shades of white, gray, and tan. It was just like in the song "Little boxes ...and they all looked just the same."

Mom's job was taking care of us and the house, keeping us clean and fed. And she bowled. Dad's job was providing the cash. They both took their jobs seriously. Mom was a clean freak and spent her days making sure the house was neat and sanitized while Dad spent countless hours at the office doing ...whatever. When Mom wasn't cleaning, she read and collected trivia like my friends' moms collected snow globes or salt and pepper shakers. I don't know what Dad was doing when he wasn't working or bowling.

Now Maggie was a "bird of a different feather." I thought she looked cool and with-it. She let her dark brown curly hair go wild and she never wore make up or nail polish, but she always wore some kind of jewelry, usually long dangly earrings or a collection of bracelets.

Unlike the neighborhood moms, Maggie *did* wear shorts, pedal pushers and pants, mostly jeans; she wouldn't be caught dead in a shirtwaist print dress. Maggie liked to sew and created many of her own outfits, especially colorful shifts and jumpers.

She was divorced (maybe marital unhappiness was inherited, some sort of defective sibling gene) and lived in this old painted farmhouse with a bunch of cats and dogs, plus a rescue pig named Peggy Sue and a goat named Buddy Holly, just outside of the little town of Miesville (population 126) on Nicolai Avenue.

When she wasn't working her garden, collecting junk, and caring for the animals, she was teaching elementary school in Hastings, the neighboring "big" town (population 9,000) and writing a bunch of essays and short stories based on her life. She'd actually "sold" a few. Cool, huh? With the alimony from her ex, her teaching salary, and the sale of the abundant produce from her garden and an occasional publishing check, she managed to support herself and remain independent. As she told me once, "Who needs a man when you can have a pig, a goat, and a garden?"

When I first saw Maggie's house, which Carrie called the Rainbow House because she just loved rainbows and the movie *Wizard of Oz*, I was kind of freaked out because it was so weird. Maggie was to spicy as Mom was to bland. Maggie would buy whatever paint was on sale and just paint until the paint ran out and then she'd change colors. Sometimes if there was a little left in the can, she'd mix it with another color to create something new.

For example, the second story was painted shades of red, from maroon, rust, to almost pink. I bet the neighbors got a kick out of that. Yeah right. Thank goodness she used only one color of yellow for the trim. But then there was the purply blue front porch, "periwinkle" according to the can. Still not too bad until you saw the spindles: pumpkin orange, lime green, and hot pink. She tied the craziness together with the yellow porch floor, which matched the trim on the windows. Yup, Aunt Maggie was the crazy lady with the Rainbow House and the zoo. We'd fit right in.

"It's my birthday not Susie's. Why is her name on the envelope?" Carrie looked at me with a frown. "It's my birthday. Can I open it? Please?" Carrie begged, jumping up and down. Carrie expected the usual $10, but I also wondered why Aunt Maggie had put my name on the card.

"Cool it, Hyper Girl, it's just a card, not an invitation to a Beatles or Elvis concert." Just the thought of the Beatles and Elvis made me go all fizzy inside. "Okay, Goofy, read the card out loud if you must. Just stop jumping up and down. Okay?"

"I must, I must," Carrie said as she ripped open the envelope.

> *Dear Kids,*
>
> *I know you just finished school and are ready to celebrate your freedom. Why not celebrate it with me? I've already okayed it with your folks and you're welcome to spend your summer with me out in the country where the air is pure and the water is clean and clear. Okay, so that's BS because of the neighbors' pig farm, but seriously I could really use your help around here.*
>
> *I'd pay you a pittance, feed you, and take you*

*to my favorite places like the lake near Cannon
Falls. The water is even pretty clear. By the way,
Suze, my neighbor is very cute and he helps
with the chores when he can. Don't freak, Sis,
I'm not trying to set her up! Just sweeten the
pie a bit. Let me know what you decide so we
can finalize plans.*

Love,

Aunt Maggie

P. S. I've added some chickens to the zoo.

"What's BS?" Carrie asked, grabbing the $10 bill and
tossing the card with the beautiful, hand-painted flock
of bluebirds on the table.

"Bee Sting, honey," Mom answered without much
thought. "Aunt Maggie has a big garden and lots of bees.
She just wants to warn you."

I was totally into a bluebird memory by this time and
tuned Mom and Carrie out. Bluebirds were a favorite
of mine with their summer sky backs and their rusty
metal bellies. The only real, honest-to-god bluebirds I'd
ever seen was when I was watching Carrie while she
was wading in the kids' pool in Hester Park. I saw a
flash of bright blue and spotted two beauties in a nearby
tree. Seeing those birds made my day.

"Well, kids, what do you think?" Mom said. "It would
be a chance to make some money and have some fun in
the process. It's a bit of a drive, about 110 miles one
way, I believe, but I could come and get you if you get
bored."

"That will be one short vacation. Bored, are you
kidding me? A summer with Aunt Maggie will take

boredom to a whole new level. There's absolutely nothing to do in Miesville, Minnesota, population 120. We've been there a few times, remember?"

"Actually the population is 126," Mom corrected as she puttered around the kitchen.

"Big whoop," I said under my breath. "What about my summer bowling league? They're going to freak when they find out their best bowler is going to be gone all summer."

"I'm sure you and your team will survive, honey. Maybe you could join a league in Hastings?"

"Fat chance they even have a bowling alley. This is Hicksville, remember?"

My family, as boring as they were, loved to bowl at the Granite Bowl, St. Cloud's only bowling alley. Mom and Dad were each in several leagues, including their couples' league. Dad was an exceptional bowler, scoring several 700 games and averaging over 200.

Mom, whose average was 135-140, just loved getting out of the house with her bowling pals. I bowled in two leagues for teenagers and averaged 160 and 155 respectively. And now I was giving up my summer league to go to Miesville, population 126. What are the chances they'd even have a bowling alley? Zip. Talk about a Bummer Summer.

"We get to go to Aunt Maggie's. We get to go to Aunt Maggie's," Carrie sang and started to jump up and down — again. "And play with all the animals and eat her blueberry pancakes." I think she was a pogo stick in a former life.

"Well, there are Maggie's blueberry pancakes and I do like all the animals."

Mom never let us have pets because they shed,

pooped, peed, and did animal things which messed up her perfect, but boring, house. "That's a plus, but we'll be doing chores, remember? That could be a real bummer. Muckin' out the barn with all that pig and goat poop."

"*Eww,*" Carrie said. "Stinky poop."

"At least she has a TV and a few bikes. If things get too bad, we can always bike to King's for their 'burgers and fries."

King's was a bar, but it wasn't just for adults. Lots of families came there with their kids, especially for the 'burgers and fries. I remember reading about its history on a plaque in the bar. The building was built in the 1870s and was a saloon, restaurant for the horse-and-buggy, snooty-patooties who needed food and rest while traveling to Red Wing.

"Or we could really live life on the edge and bike to Hastings if it's not too far."

"It's eleven miles if I remember correctly," Mom said. Mom's thing with numbers and other trivia was very annoying. A break from the family was looking more appealing by the minute.

And there was Maggie's menagerie: two dogs, a bunch of farm cats, Peggy Sue, the pig, and Buddy Holly, the goat, and now chickens. Plus she let us do practically anything we wanted and we could make a mess without her having a hissy fit. Maybe Maggie's "cute" neighbor and I could have some fun.

Yeah, right. You know you freak when boys are around. You get all shy and weird.

I need to explain something. I have these two voices inside me (or maybe it's one voice with a split personality): one is encouraging, like a coach, and the other is shaming and harsh like a crabby teacher. I wish I could tell the crabby teacher to "shut up." They always appeared when I thought about boys and dating. When I was actually around boys, these inner voices were loud and intrusive. Sometimes they even argued.

Maybe a summer at Maggie's would be a blast. At least we'd escape the Mom and Dad Wars, plus we'd get freedom, 'burgers, fries, and lots of blueberry pancakes. And I wouldn't have to endure Mom and her Bee Sting statistics. A girl could dream couldn't she?

Go for it, girl.
Not a chance!
See what I mean?

CHAPTER 2

The Arrival

June 1964

The car was hot, the drive was long, Mom's choice of music was a drag, and Carrie was a pest with her "Are we there yets?" Finally, we pulled into Maggie's long, dusty, gravel road past the wooden vegetable stand where Maggie sold her produce, jams, jellies, and pickles on Fridays, Saturdays, and Sundays.

"I can't imagine how she gets to work in the winter," Mom said.

"Maybe she skis or uses snow shoes. Maybe a dog sled," I said, rolling my eyes.

"Don't roll your eyes at me, young lady."

I rolled my eyes.

"There's the Rainbow House!" Carrie squealed and started to sing "Somewhere over the rainbow. . ."

"You have no idea how irritating that is, Sis." She continued singing.

"Oh, my goodness, she's added even more outrageous colors," Mom said. "I'll bet there are over fifty different colors in the front alone. Lord knows what the back looks like."

"Why don't you count the colors?" I said under my breath.

"One thing I won't miss is your sarcasm, young lady. Oh, my God, is that a pig in the front yard?" As soon as the car stopped, Carrie was out the door and running to get a hug from the pig and Maggie in that order.

Our arrival had now been noticed by the remaining menagerie and we were greeted by two dogs, mutts from the looks of them, Walt Disney *Lady and the Tramp* dogs is what I called them — all whiskery and wiggly. One of the pooches jumped up and nearly knocked Mom off her feet. The goat meandered from the back, munching something that looked suspiciously like one of Maggie's socks. A cat was snoozing in each of the porch rockers.

Wearing paint-spattered overalls as colorful as her house, hair flying like swirls of cotton candy, Maggie got up from a rocker and said, "Welcome to *Chez Moi!*" She smiled and opened her arms to Mom and me.

Carrie was off with the dogs, looking for Peggy Sue.

"Let me help with the luggage," Maggie said as she and I went for another load while Mom pushed a cat off a rocker and sat down to rest.

We plopped the luggage onto the large front porch. A few years before, Maggie had screened in the end of the porch so she could sit outside after dark and avoid the Minnesota state bird: the mosquito. Inside the screened portion was a porch swing with cushions made from old quilts and a small table with an oil lamp for light.

Mom went to open the front door when Maggie

yelled, "Be careful when you open the door. There's a nest of phoebes about to hatch."

Sure enough above the front door was a nest of mud and grasses with a beautiful crested brown bird on the nest. And below the front door was a mound of phoebe poop.

"They nest here every year. We've become good friends."

You'd better hope they aren't her only friends or this will be one long BS summer and that 'cute' neighbor will be just a figment of your wild imagination.

Mom grunted as she carried in some of our luggage, while Maggie and I took our turns at resting. I could tell she wasn't impressed with Maggie, her house, the animals or the phoebe nest. I wasn't impressed exactly, but I was curious about Maggie's strange life that was so different from ours.

The inside of Maggie's house was as far out and weird as the outside. No surprise there. Maggie decorated, using garage sale, estate sale, and flea market finds. There was old stuff all over the place like advertising crates that she used for end tables and magazine holders.

Old chipped Red Wing crocks functioned as waste baskets. Old clocks chimed at all hours, none of them at the right time, and faded quilts covered the couch and chairs, each with its own cat. It seemed Maggie accessorized with cats rather than throw pillows.

Now Maggie was not a gray or tan kinda girl.

The living room was an orangey, sunny, yellow and her dining room a bluish green. The table, made from an old door, topped with glass, and side by side sawhorses, was painted white. In the center of the table was an explosion of flowers and what looked like weeds, but it was beautiful.

The brightest color, though, was in the kitchen. Painted a bright lipstick red, with white appliances, copper pots hanging from an old wheel suspended from the ceiling, old factory lights above the weathered pine table, houseplants and herbs on glass shelves in front of the windows, and small bouquets of fresh flowers, the kitchen was a delightful combination of old and new. I felt immediately at home.

"Once everyone is settled, let's have some lunch," Maggie said. "I've made a salad of greens from the garden and have the ingredients for an omelet. The chickens have been very busy. And I baked blueberry muffins for the girls." My mouth was watering at the thought.

"Sounds lovely, but I have to get back home in time for supper. Thanks so much for inviting the girls." Mom picked up her purse and started looking for the car keys. "Please call if you have any questions or need me to come to take them home. Jake and I really appreciate your help. This has been a difficult time for us."

"I know. Believe me; I understand. I was hoping we could talk while the girls were getting settled."

"I don't want to talk about it just yet, but I will want to, eventually. Thanks again, Maggie. I can't tell you how much Jake and I need this time to sort things out. I'll be in touch."

By this time Carrie had come in the kitchen door, holding a baby pig. "Mom, look what I found. Isn't she beautiful? Can I keep her?"

Mom genuinely looked horrified like the time I brought home a stray kitten who barfed roundworms all over the kitchen floor. She didn't inherit the "love animals" gene.

"I see that you found Pickles, my lil' pig. She's only three months old, the runt of the litter. The farmer was going to put her down because she was so small, but I couldn't let that happen. So now Pickles will be the logo for my homemade pickles; she'll be a star. I'm intending to market them in a more commercial way not just at my vegetable stand. I'm really going to need your help, girls."

"Can I help make pickles? and feed Pickles? and eat pickles?" Carrie said with a grin. "I'd love to help."

Mom sighed. "I certainly can't compete with pickles and Pickles," Mom said as she gave each of us a big hug. Maggie looked away, giving us some privacy.

"Let me at least send you home with some muffins, a snack for the ride home." Maggie went inside for the muffins.

"Give Daddy a hug for me," Carrie said, wiping away a few tears. By this time we were all a bit teary.

"Call us when you get home," Maggie said as she handed Mom the muffins. We all watched from the front porch as our mom went home to Dad and a possible divorce.

I felt sad that our life in St. Cloud was such a mess, disappointed that my parents couldn't make their marriage work, and angry that my life was interrupted by their problems. I could only hope that Mom and Dad could find a way to make it better for all of us. For now, Carrie and I had to get settled and make our Bummer Summer tolerable.

"Come on, Carrie, let's get upstairs and unpack. Then we can have lunch, blueberry muffins — num. And I want to explore, hold Pickles, get to know Peggy Sue and Buddy Holly. What do you say?"

"Can I take Pickles to bed with me?"

"Probably not, but I bet you can convince one of those fat cats to join you." I took my little sister by the hand and we went upstairs to settle into our new life.

CHAPTER 3

Settling In

June 1964

My second floor bedroom was painted a bluebird blue with fluffy white clouds on the wall above my headboard. The room was an odd shape because of the dormers, but I liked how quirky it was, completely unlike the perfect rectangle I was used to at home.

I was lucky enough to have two windows overlooking the backyard garden. Maggie had put small bouquets of garden flowers on the white-painted dresser and night stand. The double bed was covered with a patchwork quilt of yellows, greens, and pinks — all very cheerful and upbeat. The walls were decorated with a pine mirror and two watercolors of Maggie's version of bluebirds framed in old frames painted white. The happy room was just what I needed.

I had just finished unpacking my stuff when Carrie ran into my room.

"Susie, come see my room! I love it!" She stopped in her tracks when she saw the clouds and the paintings. For just a minute she was speechless, very unusual for Carrie. "Susie, I'm naming your room the Bluebird

Room. I love your room too! Come see mine." Carrie grabbed my hand and dragged me across the hall.

I walked into a lilac painted room with a white painted dresser and a double iron bed also painted white. Carrie had a small pine mirror and several watercolors of flowers from Maggie's garden decorating the wall. Once again the bed was covered with a handmade quilt, this one in yellows, blues, reds, and greens in a flower pattern made from one inch pentagonal pieces of colorful fabric. I'd have to ask Maggie what the pattern was. She collected old quilts and was quite knowledgeable about them. "Carrie, I'm officially declaring this the Garden Room!"

"I love my Garden Room!" Carrie said while jumping up and down.

"Finish unpacking and we'll go down for lunch. I think I smell an omelet cooking."

"Okey dokey. Then can we find Peggy Sue and Pickles?"

"Deal."

Maggie was just finishing the omelets when we walked in. The table was set with a variety of dishes picked up from garage sales. Nothing matched. Mom's dishes all matched, so did the glassware, the silverware, the pots and pans. The control freak sister and the free spirit sister. Go figure.

"How do you like your rooms?"

"We love them, don't we, Carrie?"

"Sure do."

"Fabulous. I just finished painting the clouds a few days ago." Maggie put an omelet and a serving of salad on our plates. The muffins were in a basket just waiting for us to dig in.

"Can I please have a muffin?" Carrie said, using her best table manners. We ate, laughed, ate some more and then Maggie turned a little serious.

"Girls, I'm in a bit of a pickle at the moment."

Carrie giggled when she said "pickle."

"I need to sell some of my cards and watercolors to get enough money for expenses since I don't get paid over the summer. And my ex is behind in the alimony payments. So we need to hustle and sell some stuff. Want to help?"

"Sure."

"Could we sell some eggs? and some flowers?" Carrie volunteered. "I'd like to make little bouquets in bottles and jars just like you do. And I could put them in your stand out by the road along with the vegetables."

"The lettuces and radishes are ready to be picked, but I haven't really had the time to harvest much except for my own use. Let's see what old bottles and jars we can find behind the barn where the previous owners dumped their junk. With your help, we can open the vegetable stand this weekend."

"We'll need a sign for the grand opening. Can I make one?" Carrie said, catching Veggie Stand Fever.

"Sure, let's work on it tomorrow," Maggie said.

"Last time we were here, Carrie and I found some old furniture in the barn. Could we paint and decorate some of the chairs and tables?"

"I saw a TV show where some kids found berries in the woods and made jam. Maybe we could look in the woods behind the barn and pick berries."

"Great ideas, girls. That might actually work. If you're not too tired . . ."

"We're not," Carrie yelled.

"Then explore we will. Let's create some floral and furniture masterpieces."

"Don't forget the jam."

"I won't, Carrie. We'll be Scavengers! That's what we'll be! To our scavenging!" Maggie held up her glass for a toast.

"To scavenging!" Carrie and I clinked Maggie's glass.

"What's scavenging?" Carrie asked.

"You'll see as soon as the dishes are done and the pigs are in their pen. Buddy Holly is okay to roam along with the chickens and cats. The dogs go with us."

"Can I get the pigs?"

"Let me show you what to do. Peggy Sue can be a bit stubborn, but she'll follow you anywhere if you give her a banana. Pickles will follow Peggy, but she likes bananas too."

"Anna Anna bo-banna, banana," Carrie sang at the top of her lungs. Maggie joined in.

"I'll do the dishes, just to escape the singing."

"When we're done with the chores, we'll change into our scavenger clothes. Onward and upward, ladies. To the junk yard!"

"To the pigs," Carrie said, imitating Aunt Maggie's charge.

CHAPTER 4

The Scavenger Hunt

June, 3 1964

Both Carrie and I came downstairs wearing shorts, t-shirts, and tennis shoes.

"Girls, I hate to mess with your cute outfits, but you can't scavenge in those get-ups. We're going to the woods where you might encounter poison ivy or snakes and for sure mosquitoes and black flies."

"Did I hear you say snakes? Are you kidding me?" I'd never seen any snakes in the wild, only at the zoo when we went on a day trip to the Como Zoo in St. Paul. I wasn't sure how I'd deal with seeing an actual snake.

"If we see a snake, can we bring it back?"

"If we see a snake, I'm so outta here," I said.

"Relax. Most of the snakes we might see are harmless garter or corn snakes."

"*Most* of the snakes? Why not *all* of the snakes?"

"There have been a few rattlesnakes sighted near the river bluffs, but I personally haven't seen any around here. I do have a bull snake that sometimes hangs out in the garden. Snakes can't hear but they can feel vibrations. Just stomp your feet and they'll get out of your way. They're more scared of you than you are of them."

"No way, José."

"I hope you brought long pants and long sleeved tops."

We nodded.

"Wear socks with those tennis shoes. If you brought hiking boots or wellies, wear those. Suze, I think I have a pair of wellies that will fit you. *Rubber boots! Very stylish, Suze.* Carrie, you'll have to get by with tennis shoes. I'll get you both some gloves if we're going to dig in the junk yard."

"Okay, I get it. Carrie, let's get snake-proofed and junked up!"

Once appropriately dressed, we traipsed past the garden to the woods behind the barn. Maggie's property was partially fenced on the west side to keep out the neighbors' cows.

The day was warm and I was already sweating and the wellies felt insufferable. The woods looked much cooler and very inviting even if the woods were inhabited by lions, tigers, bears *and* snakes.

Maggie was in the lead, followed by Carrie who was stomping her feet and saying "Snakes, snakes, go away. Come again some other day."

The dogs and I brought up the rear. I walked, looking down, ready to run if anything slithered close by while the dogs explored, oblivious to snake-danger.

"The junk yard is straight ahead. The farmer who owns the cows has used this land for his own personal junk yard for years. I could make a fuss because it is my land, but I've found some neat old crocks out here and don't want to alienate the neighbors. Be on the lookout for berries along the fence line."

We continued walking and stomping.

"I spy with my little eye little red berries. What do I spy? Raspberries!" Carrie yelled. "Over here." Carrie ran to the bushes. "Oh, no, I forgot to stomp." She stomped. "Why are these berries black?"

"Actually, those red berries are unripe blackberries; the black ones are ripe. Give these a taste," Maggie said as she gave each of us several red berries.

We followed directions and popped the red berries into our mouths. Carrie scrunched up her face and said, *"Eww."* Those berries were bitter and puckery sour.

"Now try these," Maggie said as she gave us each a few dark blue-black berries that were sweet and delicious. "Taste the difference?"

"These are nummy," Carrie said, stuffing her face with berries. "Can we take some home?"

The bushes were thick and prickly, grabbing and snagging our clothes. A cloud of mosquitoes swarmed around our heads, attracted by our sweat.

"No whining allowed," Maggie said, as we swatted away at the bugs. "Just keep your eyes on the prize: blackberry treats." After about a half hour we had multiple mosquito bites and also an ice cream bucket full of blackberries.

"Maybe we'll get lucky and find some raspberries to make mixed-berry jam, my favorite," Maggie said. "If not, we have enough blackberries for quite a few jars or maybe blackberry crumble with ice cream."

With black-purply stained fingers and mouths, and thoughts of crumble and ice cream, we headed to the dump to look for more treasures. Along the way, Maggie showed us how to identify poison ivy.

"Leaves of three? Let them be."
"Berries white run in fright."
"Longer stems run away from them."

With the rhymes in my head, I finally felt confident that I could identify and avoid poison ivy. Maggie continued to point out various plants and fungi. I learned more botany in that walk than I ever learned in school.

We didn't need Maggie's teaching to identify the junk yard. Old fridges, stoves and other appliances were thrown randomly into a ravine along with tires, car parts, broken furniture, bikes, and other unidentifiable junk.

Going through that pile made me very nervous, but that wasn't a problem for Maggie or Carrie.

"Gloves on, ladies. No need to go into the deepest part of the ravine; we'll stick to the periphery for today. Carrie, put your bucket down and let's start digging."

Carrie made the first discovery: a blue bottle that looked like it had contained medicine in its past life. "I found a pretty bottle. Finders Keepers!"

"Good girl, Carrie. That will be very good for flowers once we clean it up. I found the two old crocks in my living room right over here," Maggie said, showing us where she formerly struck gold.

We followed her lead.

"What's this?" Maggie said as she threw aside a plastic garbage bag. "A handmade doll cradle. Looks like it's my lucky day." She handed the cradle to me and I put it with the bottle and berries.

So far I was the only one who hadn't discovered a

hidden treasure. Not wanting to lose the competition or get too far into the ravine, I continued scrounging the edges, but I spied something that looked interesting leaning against an old stove: a small blue painted old dresser. But to get at it I had to go into the ravine. I took my time, afraid I might tumble into the junk and get hurt. After several minutes of careful maneuvering, I found my "prize."

"Maggie, come look at this. This could be a keeper." When I yelled, something dark brown and furry skittered nearby. My first thought: probably a squirrel. And then another bigger brown furry thing scurried away only this time I saw its naked scaly tail — a rat! Not a squirrel, a rat!

"Don't go into the ravine, Suze. There are rats down there. Wait for me!"

"That train has left the station. I'm already down there and have spotted two rats in the last minute. Hurry up!" Maggie quickly joined me and assessed the treasure.

"You found a beauty, Suze. Looks to be original paint on that piece. Now we just have to figure out how to get it outta here. Good thing it's small. Once we get the drawers out we should be able to move it. One drawer at a time." We carefully moved three small drawers to the top without the company of rats. Maybe we scared them away. We set the three drawers with the other treasures and then returned to tackle the actual dresser. Between the two of us we got it to the top. Still no rats, but we heard them scratching and skittering.

"Don't mention the rats to Carrie, okay?" Maggie cautioned. "We wouldn't want to scare her."

"Right." When we got to our stash, Carrie was nowhere to be found.

"Carrie, come see my treasure," I yelled.

No Carrie.

"Come on, Sis. This is no time for hide-and-seek."

Still no Carrie.

I looked all around the dump and started to walk the fence line calling her name. Maggie went the opposite direction into the woods. I could hear Maggie yelling. I was beginning to panic. Where was she?

Then I heard what sounded like a cat's meowing and saw Carrie walking towards us, holding the most bedraggled cat I'd ever seen.

"She's over here," I yelled, waving as Maggie came running.

"You really scared us, Kiddo," Maggie said, giving Carrie a hug. "Where did you find the kitten?"

"I thought I saw something we might be able to sell and went into the ravine. There was a family of squirrels digging in some garbage, but I didn't want to scare them. And then I heard the kitten cry. She was hiding inside a tire. I rescued her. Can I keep her?"

Squirrels! Yeah right. Maggie looked horrified.

I said. "Let's get your kitty home safe and sound. And no, you can't keep the 'squirrels.'"

CHAPTER 5

Hidden Treasures

June, 1964

Carrie took the cat, I put the bucket of berries in the top drawer, and Maggie took the other two drawers. We planned to come back in the morning for the dresser. The poor kitty was our top priority.

"You know, I got my other cats just this way, kids. When you live in the country, people sometimes dump their animals when they no longer want them or they don't spay or neuter their pets and they continue to have litters and the kittens become strays and have more kittens. It goes on and on."

"If Mom were here she'd give us some statistics about the number of litters a female cat can have."

Maggie nodded, used to Mom's weirdness. "A lot of people feel that cats are survivors, and some of them are, but some of them, like this poor kitty, are too young or too sick to fend for themselves. She looks to be three or four months old. It's sad."

"So how did you get Peggy Sue and Buddy Holly?" I asked.

"Interesting story. I had a college acquaintance who

converted to Buddhism and formed a group called S.L.O.P. (Stop Loathing Our Pigs). Why she focused on pigs and not cows, chickens, or any other animal I have no idea.

She 'adopted' the runt from a litter to use as a mascot and named her Peggy Sue. Then when living with a pig became problematic, she had to find a home for her and someone told her about me. Bam, instant pig owner. She's actually been quite delightful, so much so that I adopted another runt pig as a companion for her."

"And Buddy Holly, the goat? Will you get a companion for him too?"

"Good lord, no. I found him wandering the dirt road last year. I went into town and put up notices, but no one claimed him. Now I understand why: He's an escape artist. When I first rescued him, I confined him to his stall in the barn. The next morning he was out in the front yard, snacking on my zinnias. I should have called him Houdini. He's actually a bit of a nuisance, eating whatever he darn well pleases! But he does keep down the weeds in the pasture."

When we got back to the Rainbow House, Maggie gave the cat a small amount of food and water on the front porch (we didn't want the cat to barf) before she examined her. Other than being really hungry and dirty, she looked skinny but okay. She was so dirty she looked like a Halloween witch's familiar. No drippy eyes or any other indication of disease that we could see.

"She probably has worms and maybe fleas, so we'll give her a flea bath just in case. I have an extra flea collar we can use after the bath. I'll worm her in the morning. We don't want to freak her out. Right now she's so grateful to have food and some attention she's happy just to be here. Listen to her loud purr. Any idea what we should name her?"

"How about Motor Boat 'cause she sounds like a motor boat?"

"Maybe? Evenrude, Johnson or Mercury?" Maggie suggested, which got a laugh from me and a questioning look from Carrie.

"Those are names of outboard motors, Carrie."

"How about Phyllis? She's my best friend at school and sometimes she needs a bath, just like the kitty."

"Hmm, Phyllis, I like that," I said.

"I've got it!" Carrie squealed. "Blackberry 'cause today we found so many of them."

"I think we should wait until after her bath. We might be surprised at what color her fur is."

"Don't cats hate water?"

"Most cats do, though I had a tough old Tom that loved drinking from the lawn sprinkler. He'd get pretty wet and then shake himself off like a dog. To be on the safe side, we'll wear gloves. She's weak and probably won't fight too much."

Yeah right. For such a skinny, weak kitty, she fought like a tiger, scratching us through our long-sleeved shirts. There were soap suds all over the lawn and ourselves. Eventually she tired herself out and let us rinse and dry her. She didn't even resist when Maggie put on the flea collar.

Carrie found an old cardboard box in the garage and Maggie gave her a stack of clean old towels and blankets for the kitten's bed. Covering a corner of the box with a towel to make a kitty fort "'cause kitties like their privacy," Carrie put the box and the kitty into the screened porch.

After a few cat treats, Miss Unnamed Kitty turned around a few times and curled up. By the time I'd gone upstairs for Band-Aids and Merthiolate for our scratches, the kitten was sound asleep in her bed. Maggie had an old cake pan that she filled with sand in case the kitty needed to use the bathroom.

"Poor little thing. She's exhausted. When she wakes up, we'll give her more food and water. Let's try to keep the adult cats inside until tomorrow. We don't want to scare her. And we don't want the other cats to get fleas, if she still has them.

Can you believe she's actually white with black spots? I would have bet the farm that she was black or gray. She was absolutely filthy. Once she's rested, I'll check her for fleas. They should be easy to spot with her white coat."

"So Motor Boat, Phyllis and Blackberry are in the running for kitty's name," I said to Carrie. "I'm going to add another to the list. The black spots around her face and over her butt remind me of Snoopy."

"I love Charlie Brown and Snoopy, but I love Blackberry more. She's my cat and I get to name her whatever I want," Carrie said, letting us know that she *would* get her way.

Stubborn, persistent and spoiled, she almost always got what she wanted. Once she got mad at me for something and gave me the silent treatment for three days, which I loved, by the way. She did the same thing with Mom and Dad, but, unlike me, they didn't enjoy the silence. Instead they worried about her and would eventually give in. She was the queen of manipulation.

"No arguments there, Sis."

"Maybe we should decide in the morning. We'll keep her in the screened porch, so she doesn't run off," Maggie said.

"I'm gonna sleep on the porch swing so she knows I love her and want her to stay."

"Let's talk about sleeping arrangements after supper. How about 'burgers on the grill and potato chips? Something easy."

"Can we have ice cream with blackberries for dessert? In honor of Blackberry, my new best friend."

"Sure thing, sweetie. Blackberry sundaes for dessert."

Carrie gave me a I-won-that-argument grin. The kid was on a roll. If I know Carrie, she'd also be sleeping on the porch swing with her new best friend purring beside her.

CHAPTER 6

Sweet Revenge

June, 1964

While Maggie and I were comfortable in our beds, I hoped Carrie would be uncomfortable in the porch swing. Maggie and I both woke up on the right side of the bed while Carrie woke up on the wrong side of the porch swing. Sweet.

Maggie and I were sitting in the kitchen, having toast and orange juice when Crabby Carrie sauntered in, with her hair sticking up and a scab on her nose, carrying an equally crabby, squirmy cat under her arm.

"Looks like you had a tough night," Maggie said. I grinned.

"Blackberry jumped on the swing and kept me awake almost all night with her purring. Once she attacked my nose and then she did this really stinky poop that woke me up." I laughed and Carrie glared and said, "Meanie, meanie, cocoa beanie."

That's what she always said when she thought I was mocking her. It was deserved mockery.

By this time, the house cats had meandered in, curious about the new addition.

Not to be left out of the crabby vibe, Blackberry looked at them and hissed.

"Before we let her meet the other cats, let's take her back to the porch to check on the possible flea situation," Maggie said. "I'll bring her food out there."

Carrie grumbled but did what she was told for a change.

"Looks like we dodged a bullet; I couldn't see any evidence of fleas, not to say that we won't see any later. The bath and collar must have worked their magic."

"Thank goodness."

Carrie came into the kitchen holding the smelly cake pan. "What do I do with this?"

"Take it behind the barn and dump it. There's a pile of sand by the garden. You'll have to do this every day she stays on the porch."

Carrie groaned.

"If you're going to claim the kitty, you need to learn how to take care of her, so no whining allowed. It won't be long before she'll go outside to do the stinkies."

Wow! Maggie was insisting that my spoiled sister should actually do some chores. Radical! Carrie managed to weasel out of them at home and still get an allowance. Mom made her bed, washed and folded her clothes, and even made her lunch because the Princess didn't like school lunch.

Can't say I blame her for that, but she could at least make her own lunch and her own bed once in a while. Maybe Maggie could teach her a few things about responsibility and consequences. I could only hope.

"I used the hose to rinse it out and then I put in fresh sand like you said." That comment blew my mind. She might actually come around.

"Good. You're learning, sweetie. Did Berry like her breakfast?"

"She gobbled it down and then attacked me, but she didn't bite hard."

"You girls have a lot to learn about cats. Kittens eat, play, and get into mischief"

"And do poop-stinkies."

"Don't we all. All she needs are some toys to occupy her. After breakfast we'll see what we can find in the barn."

"My friend, Phyllis, has a kitty and she has this feather toy that her cat really likes. We could collect some chicken feathers and find a bendy stick. I bet that would work," she said with enthusiasm.

I was expecting Carrie to flip out and start jumping like the jumping bean she was; instead she ran out the back, slamming the screen door as she went.

"And she's off!"

"Don't forget Berry!" Maggie yelled, but Carrie was already in the barn. "I think we should keep Berry on the porch for a few days until she knows this is her forever home," Maggie said, picking up the cat. "You bring the kitty potty. Once she gets a little older and gets to roam the farm, she'll find her own toys like mice, birds, bugs. I once had a cat that brought home baby garter snakes."

"Enough with the snakes, Maggie."

"You'll get used to them eventually. They're really good to have around the farm; they keep down the rodents and slugs."

"Slugs? No way." I paused, imagining how a snake would eat a slug. *Gross.* "You sure know a lot about animals and plants. Have you ever taught biology? You should, you know."

"When you teach second grade, you teach a little bit of everything."

"Have you always taught second grade?"

"My first few years were with fifth graders and I liked them too, but I found I had more fun with the younger kids."

"That shows with Carrie. You're really good with her. I sometimes forget that she's still a little kid."

By the time we returned to the kitchen, Carrie had found several feathers and a bendy stick. She barged into the kitchen, slamming the door once again. "Will these work?"

"They sure will. We can make the toys after you have some breakfast. Help yourself to the cereal on the counter and the blackberries in the fridge. While you're having breakfast, I have chores to do: slop the hogs and all that. Why don't you join Suze and me out in the barn when you're done eating. Suze, don't forget your wellies; you'll be helping to muck out the stalls."

"Should I bring a clothes pin for my nose. It's pretty stinky out there."

"You'll get used to it, City Girl."

Now the barn had yet to be Rainbowized, but I had no doubt it would be in the future. No barn red for Maggie. Maybe a lime green with periwinkle stripes or polka dots. Other than needing a good coat of paint, the barn seemed to be well-built and maintained.

The four chickens had their coop inside the barn, but were allowed to roam free in the yard most of the time. Same with Peggy Sue and Pickles. Buddy Holly was a bit of a badass goat and did whatever he pleased, sorta like Carrie now that I thought about it.

"Maggie, do all the animals get along?"

"Yup. We're all love and peace in the barn, especially in the winter when they're confined. I fire up the wood stove if it's really cold and make sure they have lots of dry, clean hay, good food, and fresh water."

"I can't believe how much you have to do around here. What time do you get up in the morning anyway?"

"When I'm teaching, around four. Otherwise around five-thirty or six."

"Seriously? And I complain about getting up at six."

"I get some help from Eric, my 17-year-old neighbor from down the road. He gets here around five-thirty and finishes the chores while I shower and make us breakfast. Then it's off to school. Eric is a real life-saver; I don't think I could live out here on my own without his help. You'll meet him this afternoon when he comes to mow the yard and help in the garden."

I tried to wrap my brain around Maggie's Peaceable Kingdom and thought about our unpeaceable home and how Mom and Dad could learn from the pigs, chickens, and billy goat.

And then there was Eric, the "cute" neighbor Maggie mentioned in her card who was coming this afternoon. I was about to enter my favorite teenage romantic fantasy when one of the dogs sauntered into the barn, spied the red chicken, and started to chase her.

"So much for peace and harmony," Maggie said, laughing. "The red chicken is Mrs. Minniver and she's a real character. Every morning these two play tag and the Mrs. usually wins."

Sure enough "the Mrs." chased the dog into the yard.

"You should see her when she rides on Peggy Sue's back."

"Doesn't Peggy Sue mind?"

"She actually loves a good scratch. So do I, now that I think about it."

Just then Carrie ran into the barn, dragging Berry's new toy on the ground with Berry in hot pursuit. "She really likes her new toy. Watch this."

Carrie held the toy just a few feet above Berry's head; she stood on her hind legs and batted the feather. Then Berry spied the real deal and the chase was on.

When "the Mrs." had had enough, she turned and took the offensive. Berry didn't have a chance.

"You should probably keep an eye out for your kitten. You don't want her wandering off somewhere."

"She'll be okay. I wanna look for treasures in the barn. Remember I found the first treasure in the dump." Carrie looked all self-satisfied and smug, the little brat.

"The good stuff is in the hay loft, but wait for us, Carrie, so I can show you where to look. We're almost done here."

"Too late, Maggie. She's off and running."

I looked up to see Carrie climbing a very unsteady ladder. Time slowed down and I watched my little sister climb the ladder half way to the hay loft, lose her balance, wave her arms and fall ... right into Buddy Holly's stall, the only one we hadn't yet mucked out.

Somewhere between a thunk and splat we found an uninjured Carrie looking stunned and embarrassed. With hay and muck sticking to her hair and clothes like feathers, Little Miss Know-It-All started to howl. Just then Berry trotted into the stall and deposited a very dead mouse at Carrie's feet.

"Ah, a present from your new best friend," I said with a grin.

CHAPTER 7

The Meeting

June, 1964

"Maggie, I'm going to run a bath for lil' Sis and see that's she's cleaned up. A bath and a nap, how about it?" I put my arm around her skinny shoulders as we walked.

"Good luck with that. I'll be in after I finish out here."

Waiting until Maggie couldn't hear, Carrie said, "I'm not a baby and I don't take naps! And I can run my own bath and wash my own hair. You aren't the boss of me."

She pushed my arm away and stomped up to the house, like she was trying to scare off snakes and I was the snake.

Back home when she'd throw a snit fit, I'd let her cool off on her own, so, hoping this strategy would work here, I walked up the driveway to the road along with the dogs. Where did Eric live anyway? I hope he's nice-looking.

Admit it, girl, you want a hunky, gorgeous guy with dimples. I know you.

It had to be near by, but after about a ten minute walk, I didn't see any houses and went back to check on Carrie. *Bummer.*

The large family bath was upstairs and hadn't yet been remodeled, but it did have Maggie's personal touches like the old lace tablecloth she used for a shower curtain, an antique dresser for storage and a dilapidated wicker rocker. Seriously, a chair in a bathroom? I suppose if you had a young kiddo who needed watching, it might make sense. Carrie was having a fine time splashing away. I didn't need to watch her, but I sat in the chair anyway.

"You don't need to watch me, Carrie. I like my privacy, too, you know."

"Okay, kid, I can take a hint."

Since I was about to meet "cute" guy, I thought I needed a bit of cleaning up myself, so after Carrie kicked me out, I headed for the half bath off the kitchen. Maggie and I share the same hair, only she lets her curls go natural. I've tried the Jackie Kennedy flip, but it just doesn't work.

Guess I'm my mother's child 'cause I couldn't quite go for the out-of-control look, so I wet down my curls and re-braided. I washed my face and wished that I could get rid of the freckles across my nose.

Who's gonna look twice at a tall, skinny girl with outta control hair and freckles?

At least my teeth were straight and I liked my ears. Oh, and my feet, I liked them, too, cause they were long and skinny and I could pick stuff up with my toes. *Sad that your ears and feet are your best features.* A change of clothes and I would be ready to meet Eric. Just as I was about to go upstairs to change and check on Carrie, I heard a knock on the front screen door. Rats!

"Anybody home?" Through the screen door I spied a tall, thin, red-haired boy with freckles, crooked teeth, huge feet, and ears that stuck out. *You might be in luck, girl. He's tall, sorta skinny and has freckles, too.* He was wearing an old t-shirt and faded jeans.

When he saw me, he grinned, flashing me the most adorable dimples which canceled the big ears. *Gotta love those dimples.* The feet would take getting used to.

"You must be Eric. Maggie is in the barn."

"Thanks." And he left. Gone. No conversation, no introduction, no "Nice to meet you."

Way to go, Suze. Way to engage. You dummy, you didn't even tell him your name. You're hopeless. No surprise. Face it — you're uptight around boys. Wait, there was the group date in 8th grade with a boy named Tucker that rhymed with you-know-what and it wasn't Pucker. All you remember is he had pimples and smelled of onions. That's it, your dating history. Pathetic.

When I walked upstairs, I checked the bathroom and no Carrie. I cleaned out the tub of Carrie debris and checked her bedroom. She had put on her pjs and was curled up with one of Maggie's house cats. After her bad night she needed a nap. When I looked at her all clean and innocent, I melted. Poor kid. She must be exhausted and homesick.

I changed my clothes and got ready to help Maggie make the blackberry crumble. Sure enough she was already in the kitchen. I could hear the sound of the lawnmower accompanying Nancy Wilson's version of "The Very Thought of You."

Maggie was singing along as she prepared the dessert.

"The crumble should be done just in time for lunch. We're having tuna salad sandwiches, chips and lots of pickles. I thought you kids could help me figure out which kind would be the best sellers. We need to start making plans for the Pickle Project. Eric will be joining us, by the way." I could feel my face getting hot, thinking about what a chicken I was, scared to talk to Eric, any boy actually. *Suze's getting nervous, Suze's getting nervous.*

"Would you mind picking some leaf lettuce for the sandwiches? Beware of Ernie, the bull snake." When she saw me pale, she added, "Don't freak. I was just joking. Haven't seen Ernie for a couple of years." So I stomped my way to the garden just in case.

While I was picking greens, I saw Eric get off the riding lawn mower and walk toward me. *You can do this. You can do this.*

"Hey, you! Need some help?"

Just breathe and answer his question. "No, thanks, I'm almost done here. See you in a few minutes." *Way to go. You did it! Not exactly the coolest conversation, but at least you talked to him.*

When I got back into the kitchen, Maggie was setting the table and I could smell the crumble baking. Eric was sitting at the table, chatting comfortably with Maggie about afternoon chores.

"When I finish mowing, I'll start in the garden."

"Sounds good. The girls and I will be out in the barn looking for furniture to paint. We're planning a little Artsy-Fartsy sale sometime in August. By the way, we're opening the veggie stand this Friday. Spread the word. Suze, I'm going to check on Carrie. The timer for the crumble should go off in about fifteen minutes. Please take it out of the oven." She looked at me and winked.

Great, you're alone with Eric and are tongue-tied.

After what seemed a very long time, I decided to go for it and ask him some questions. He evidently had the same idea because we both started to talk at the same time. Then we laughed — together. *You're in sync, a good sign, Suze.* Finally, I said, "You go first."

"Okay. You wouldn't happen to like baseball would you?"

Should you lie and say you love it or should you tell the truth. If you lie you'll get caught. You always do.

"Not so much, but I did go to a few St. Cloud Rox games. My dad is the baseball fan in the family. He loves both Harmon Killebrew and Tony Oliva. He makes us listen to the games on the radio. I kinda tune 'em out though."

"Cool. Okay, your turn to ask a question."

"Where do you live anyway? I took a walk this morning and couldn't see any houses close by."

"My dad and I live off US 61 so you wouldn't see our house from here."

No Mom. Wonder what happened there. Don't ask. Wait for him to bring it up.

"When the weather's nice, I bike over. In the winter, I drive."

"Maggie told me about how much you help her."

"I do what I can. I like earning some money and she's a great cook. Besides, I like the animals."

Hmm, appreciates money, good food, animals and probably baseball. You might actually have a chance with this one.

"You have your license! I'm impressed. Mom and Dad won't even think about letting me get my permit let alone a license. You are so lucky."

"Yeah, lucky me," he said, but he said it kinda like he was sad. "My mom died two years ago. She had cancer."

Now what do you say? Duh, how about sorry?

"Sorry. That must be hard."

"Yeah, but it's getting easier...." Eric paused to

compose himself. "Dad coaches the Mudhens and I play on the team. We're playing this Saturday if you want to come watch."

Could this be a date? Nah, don't jump the gun, girl.

Just then Carrie and Maggie came into the kitchen, Carrie, wearing her jammies and carrying a cat. "What's for lunch? I'm super hungry."

"I've made tuna salad. Carrie, why don't you help me make the sandwiches. Be sure to wash your hands first."

"I just had a bath, Aunt Maggie."

"But you were snuggled up with a kitty." Maggie went to the fridge to take out the tuna salad, pickles, and just-picked greens. Carrie washed her hands, then wiped them on her pjs.

"What now?"

"The bread is in the bread box and the chips are in the cupboard to the right of the sink."

"I can't reach the chips or the breadbox," Carrie said as she started to move a chair to the counter. Then she saw Eric. "Who are you?"

"Carrie, this is Eric and he helps me with chores like mowing the lawn." Carrie looked at me and then at Eric.

"Is he going to be your boyfriend, Suze?" I could feel myself blushing.

"How about if I get the chips and bread for you and we'll make sandwiches together," I said, trying not to embarrass myself.

Good save, girl. You're catchin' on.

"I can do it myself." Carrie dragged the chair to the counter, talking all the way. "I'm making our sandwiches for lunch. I'm learning to cook like Aunt Maggie. We're going to make pickles to sell and we're finding treasures to sell because Maggie is broke and doesn't have enough money, but we're helping. Right Maggie? If you're going to be Suze's boyfriend, you have to help, too."

Eric smiled. "I can do that."

CHAPTER 8

The Plan

June ,1964

"Family meeting, that includes you, too, Eric, at three. We need to come up with a plan for Friday's opening. Advertising, inventory, preparation, work schedules, who's responsible for what. Everybody clear on that?"

"You betcha!" I said and everybody agreed.

"I'm off to finish the lawn. Thanks for the lunch, Maggie." As we walked out to the garden, Eric said, "Why do I feel like I just volunteered for the army and this is boot camp?"

"Because that's exactly what it is and Maggie is the drill sergeant. All that's missing is the salute. I'm going to check out the hay loft for treasures. See you at three."

"That's 1500 hours, ma'am," Eric said with a grin. *Those dimples, girl, no wonder you're smitten.*

"I am not smitten," I said aloud.

"What did you say?"

"I said, 'I should have worn mittens.'" *Now he'll think you're nuts. Nice move.* Eric just shook his head.

Maggie and Carrie joined me in the barn after Carrie changed clothes and Maggie did the dishes. By this time

I was already in the loft and had found absolutely nothing of value unless hay counts.

I received my orders: furniture and containers for flowers. I hadn't found anything because I didn't know where to look. There were nooks and crannies everywhere filled with what appeared to be garbage, but Maggie saw things differently. She showed us where she had found things in the past, so we started there.

Mainly there were boxes of stuff shoved back against the walls, many of them covered with hay. It was just a matter of looking in the boxes. We pulled out a box for each of us and started to explore. I was just a little nervous because there might be mice or other critters hanging out in the contents. All of a sudden Carrie let out a squeal. Maybe she found the critters.

"I found Treasures. Dishes and newspaper." Maggie and I walked over to examine the treasures. I found myself more interested in the papers than the dishes, but you can't sell old newspapers, even if they are over twenty years old, especially when they were used for packing.

As we unwrapped the dishes, we discovered they were mostly chipped, but there were several cups and saucers in a rose and ivy pattern that could be used for bouquets. Then Maggie found a chipped tea pot that she just loved. "Maybe we could make something from the chipped dishes, a mosaic perhaps. Keep looking, ladies."

After an hour we had "harvested" several patterned table cloths that the mice hadn't chewed, a pair of old wooden ice skates, a handmade sled, some housedresses from the thirties that Maggie wanted to re-purpose as throw pillows, an old oil lamp, and several broken chairs. Quite a haul!

Once we got everything down, we could actually evaluate the junk. It had looked better in the dim lighting of the loft, but Maggie looked anything but discouraged. She was flyin' high!

"These will be perfect for our Artsy-Fartsy sale. Now we have to figure out what we're going to sell Friday. Busy, busy. Are we having fun yet?"

I had to admit we were. Carrie was having the time of her life and so was I.

At 1300 hours we were gathered around the kitchen table, all sweaty and dirty from our afternoon adventures. *Girl, you are one ugly mess.*

"Can we wash up first? I itch all over from the hay," Carrie whined. "I get the downstairs bathroom."

"I'll take the laundry room."

"And I'll use the hose outside," Eric said.

"That leaves the upstairs for me," I said.

By the time I got downstairs, Maggie had made cherry Kool-Aid and set out a plate of sugar cookies. That gave me an idea for this coming weekend: We could sell Kool-Aid and cookies. That would be a great job for Carrie. Little did I know that Maggie had much bigger plans.

"Now that we all feel a little better let's brainstorm this Friday's opening. I'll take some notes. First, we need to make some signs that we can post at King's, Wiederholdt's, the gas station, and along Nicolai Ave. We'll need at least ten signs.

"What's a Wiederholdt's?" Carrie asked.

"It's a supper club, honey," Maggie said.

"Do we want to advertise in Hastings?" Eric asked.

Girl, did you notice he used the pronoun we? Lookin' good.

"I never have, but it wouldn't hurt. Maybe we could put that on hold until after our opening. If we don't get many people, we might have to branch out. The season always starts out slowly."

"When we make the signs, we should list what we're selling which brings me to inventory. I've been thinking. We have tons of rhubarb; it's free, not very labor intensive to harvest."

"Doesn't everybody have rhubarb? Why would ours be special?"

"Because we'd make it special. Rhubarb muffins, rhubarb coffee cake, rhubarb crisp, rhubarb jam, rhubarb custard pies. What we don't sell this weekend we could freeze. We'll start small to see what our customers like and then we can adjust."

"What about flowers?" I asked.

"I want to do flowers," Carrie said, "because I found that pretty blue bottle."

"What flowers are available? I love the bouquets you've made, but you've included more than flowers. There are branches, shrubs, grasses, a whole bunch of stuff I'd never think of including in a bouquet."

"Well, we've got peonies, pansies, bleeding hearts, bridal wreath, and lots of wild flowers. When we're done here, we'll check out the fields along the road. I've seen butterfly weed and some daisy like yellow flowers, I don't know what they're called. Anything is fair game. Again, we'll have to see what sells.

"Flowers are tricky because they're fragile. We'll pick the flowering shrubs and grasses in the evening and put them in water in the barn. That means we'll be picking the garden and wild flowers and making bouquets early in the morning. Eric, what's ready to harvest in the garden?"

"Spinach, leaf lettuce, radishes, green onions, and peas are just beginning to produce. Oh, and we have strawberries, not a lot, but some."

"I also have some jams and jellies from last fall I could put out."

"I have a game on Saturday night so I can't work past two, but I'm available Friday and Sunday." Eric looked at me.

I picked up on it. "I want to go to the game Saturday night. Can I go?"

"I think we should all go to the game, maybe have 'burgers at King's to celebrate, if we're not too tired."

"It's a date," Eric said. "See you tomorrow at 0900 hours." Then he winked at me. Unreal.

Did you hear that, girl? You've got yourself a wink and a date.

Chapter 9

The Grand Opening

June, 1964

The next two days were a blur of activity: making and putting up signs, cleaning up and decorating the stand, buying supplies for baking, and harvesting the radishes, onions, rhubarb, asparagus and peas. The fragile strawberries, lettuces and spinach would have to be last minute, along with the flowers.

We'd scouted the woods, fields, and yard for anything we could use. We'd also been saving our change, but Maggie went to the bank to get ones and quarters just in case.

Then we started baking. Maggie got out Grandma's cook book and found several recipes that would work. Maggie couldn't exactly follow the recipes without adding some of her own ideas, so we made rhubarb muffins with a dollop of strawberry jam in the middle as a surprise. The rhubarb cake had a cinnamon, brown sugar, butter and chopped walnut topping, my favorite.

We also made rhubarb bread. The kitchen smelled amazing. By Thursday night we were pretty much exhausted. Eric left after eating half a loaf of rhubarb bread and Carrie had fallen asleep with her head on the kitchen table.

"The muffins look beautiful on those dinner plates and saucers we found," I said. "Our customers are getting delicious food plus a pretty plate, even if they have some chips." We covered the plates and saucers with plastic wrap to keep everything fresh and moist and to protect them from snoopy, hungry cats, especially Berry who loved to get into everything.

"What's the weather forecast for tomorrow and the weekend?" Maggie said. "I've been too busy to check."

"According to the radio, we have a slight chance of rain tomorrow and Saturday with possible thunderstorms late Saturday and all day on Sunday. If we get two good days out of three we'll be lucky. I just hope Eric's game doesn't get rained out."

"Me, too." Maggie yawned. "Our work here is done, at least until Eric gets here around six tomorrow morning. He'll pick the strawberries, lettuces and spinach and we'll work with the flowers. Are the containers ready and clean?"

"Yup, they're in the barn, filled with water ready to go. I've picked some shrubs, grasses, Queen Anne's lace and they're already in water. We just have to gather the flowers and make the arrangements."

"Let's call it a night. You get Carrie and I'll check on the animals to make sure they're settled in. We'll have to keep the chickens, pigs and Buddy Holly in the barn tomorrow. I wouldn't want them to follow us to the stand and get hit by a car. The dogs and cats will be okay. Thanks for everything, sweetie. You're the best." Maggie gave me a big hug.

I woke up Carrie and led her upstairs. I don't think

she was ever fully awake because she let me tuck her in without protest.

Five-thirty came awfully early. I was too wound up with thoughts of Eric and the grand opening to get much sleep.

Admit it, girl, you're smitten.

Maybe I am. He's the first guy I've ever been around where I've actually felt comfortable. I can talk to him and he talks to me. If that's what smitten means, I'm smitten. He seemed awfully nice. Next year will be his senior and my junior year. Who knows? Maybe Carrie and I will spend another summer with Maggie. I wouldn't mind that at all. A quick shower and I was ready for our busy day. Carrie was still sound asleep. I could hear Maggie downstairs talking to Eric and making tea. She sliced some more rhubarb bread for a quick breakfast.

After we finished eating, Eric went to harvest the vegetables in the garden while Maggie and I picked peonies, bleeding heart, pansies, the last few iris, and some yellow and blue wildflowers. We made as many arrangements as we could to fill the tea cups, the tea pot, the bottles, and pint canning jars; we added fillers of bridal veil, Queen Anne's lace, and some late blooming lilacs. Then we loaded them in a wagon and took them to Maggie's roadside stand.

When Maggie first moved to Miesville, she scavenged from Hastings to Cannon Falls and Red Wing to furnish her house.

In her search, she found some discarded bleachers from a Red Wing elementary school and knew that she would use them for her vegetable and flower stand. She painted them bright green. She asked a friend from her elementary school to build on an addition to the bleachers that she used as her work space where she stored produce and handled the cash. A green and white striped awning provided shade for the flowers. We placed all our arrangements on the top shelf of the bleachers away from the sun, if the sun came out, and headed back for another load.

By this time Eric had picked and washed the produce. We gathered Maggie's collection of baskets and vintage tea towels to display the veggies and headed back to the stand.

"Hey, wait for me. I want to make some bouquets, too!" Carrie yelled with Berry closely following. I quickly took out my arrangement from Carrie's blue bottle and stuffed the flowers into another container.

"Here you go, Sis. Your blue bottle awaits you."

"I see some pretty orange flowers in the ditch." And Carrie was off collecting butterfly weed that actually would be perfect for the blue bottle.

"When you're done, Sis, we'll help Maggie bring up the baked goods." With the baked goods arranged and looking fabulous we were open for business. And just then a black pickup truck parked along the road, driven by a very attractive man who introduced himself as Nick.

"Hi, Dad. What are you doing here?"

I was suddenly nervous and tongue-tied. *Easy girl, meeting Daddio doesn't necessarily mean he's going to propose.* I brushed off my t-shirt, wiped my hands on my shorts, and smiled.

"I wanted to sample that rhubarb bread you were raving about." He took a sample and grinned— dimples, just like Eric's. "My compliments to the chef."

"That would be me with a little help from my friends," Maggie said, pointing to Eric, Carrie, and me. "Nice to meet you, Nick. I've heard so much about you."

"Likewise. Eric tells me how hard you work to keep this little farm of yours afloat."

"Eric has been such a big help. I don't think I could do this by myself. Thanks for sharing him."

"The pleasure is all mine. You're quite a fine baker and gardener too, I see." Just then Buddy Holly walked up the road, munching grass along the way. Then Peggy Sue and Pickles meandered our direction. How did they get out?

"You'll have to excuse me. The beasts have escaped," Maggie said, laughing.

"Before you go, I'll take a loaf of the bread, a plate of muffins, a bunch of asparagus and that fantastic blue bottle with the orange flowers." Nick gave me the money and I put his purchases in a paper bag.

"I found the bottle and made the bouquet," Carrie said as she jumped up and down. "I help too!"

"I can see you're a big help, young lady."

"Thanks, Nick," Maggie said, "but I really have to go. I don't want anything to happen to my animal pals."

"I understand," Nick said. And he winked. He winked at Maggie. *Don't get stoked, girl, it might be a hereditary tic.*

CHAPTER 10

The Creep

June ,1964

By the end of the day, we'd sold out of all the baked goods, most of the flowers, and most of the veggies which meant we'd be working late. Maggie would bring some of the jams and jellies left from last fall, so we'd have some new products to sell on Saturday. I was looking forward to our dinner tomorrow at King's and then the game to follow, if the weather cooperated. According to the radio, there was a seventy percent chance of thunderstorms mostly after 6 p.m. I just hoped the weather held for our sale tomorrow and for Eric's game with the Red Wing Aces.

* * *

"I'm stuffed," Maggie said as she ate another French fry. Carrie burped in agreement. King's was a great pig-out place.

King's 'burgers, fries, and onion rings were legendary all around the area. If you visited Miesville, you ate at King's. Eat there or be square. The 'burgers were generous and grilled to perfection. With a slice of tomato, fried onion, lettuce, and homemade pickle along with crisp and salty fries, you experienced a bit of heaven. It was my favorite restaurant, better than anything in St. Cloud.

There were only two restaurants in Miesville: King's and Wiederholt's. King's was where you went for casual, every day comfort food, and Wiederholt's was for special occasions like anniversaries, birthdays, and holidays.

Wiederholt's boasted tablecloths, cloth napkins, candles, relish trays, steaks, seafood and a price tag to match while King's had paper baskets for the food served by old, sassy waitresses with dyed hair and red lips.

The wooden booths and tables were scarred from cigarettes and teenagers carving hearts and the initials of their current heart-throbs.

Ripped red vinyl seats, mismatched tables and chairs, ketchup and mustard bottles on tables instead of candles, old neon signs instead of art work decorated the working man's bar and family restaurant. Some day maybe I'd experience the fancy stuff. I did have a birthday coming up in a month. On second thought, make it King's.

"I can't believe that we sold all of our baked goods again. Does that mean we spend next week baking?"

"Afraid so," Maggie said. "We'll also have to check the barn for more dishes."

"Another scavenger hunt! Yay," Carrie said.

"Since we sold all the muffins, I assume they also liked the plates, even though they were chipped. People like to feel like they're getting a deal, something extra, ya know. They were equally jazzed about the tea cup bouquets."

"I have to go potty, Suze," Carrie said, still munching on her 'burger. "Stay here. I can go myself."

"I know you can, Sis, but I have to go, too. We might as well go together."

On our way to the restroom, we noticed a group of loud and obnoxious young guys in a booth toward the back. They had just finished eating and were concentrating on finishing the several pitchers of beer still on the table. A tall dark-haired guy dressed in red and white, the Aces' colors, yelled as I walked past, "Hey, Babe, nice rack." Then he whistled.

Everyone at the table laughed.

He got up and started toward me and Carrie. The faster we walked, the faster he walked. Then he grabbed my arm.

"Back off, jerk," I said as I pulled away.

"Slow down, babe. I just wanna talk to you."

"We don't wanna talk to you and I'm not a 'babe.' Ignore the creep, Carrie." We continued to walk and he continued to follow, pretending he needed to use the Men's.

"Come on, Ace, give it a rest," one of Ace's buddies yelled. "We don't wanna get kicked outta here, not before the game." What are the chances that the Redwing Aces would have a fan named Ace? Go figure.

"What's going on here?" Maggie said as she walked up to us, wearing her usual jeans and baggy print shirt and her signature long dangly earrings.

"Beats me," Ace said, pulling out a cigarette. "Hey, ain't you the weird broad with the vegetable stand?"

Ace stared at Maggie like a stray dog being offered some food. By this time, the bartender/bouncer, a big, burly dude, heard the commotion and intervened.

"Pay up and get outta here, boys. I've told you twice before: If you can't behave like gentlemen, I don't want to see your ugly faces in here again. Three strikes you're out. Have I made myself clear?"

"Chill, big guy, we're just leavin', ain't we boys? Hey, Butch, pay the bill."

"But our beer ... and why do I always get stuck with the bill?"

"Cause you're a pussy," Ace said and the group laughed. "Your Mudhens ain't got a chance tonight," Ace yelled at the bartender and sauntered out the door with his posse close behind.

"Thanks for your help," Maggie said to the bartender.

"I've had enough of these punks. Sorry they came on to your niece."

"Sure hope we don't run into them again," I said, still holding Carrie's hand. She looked scared and about to cry. "They're just stupid bullies. I hope the Mudhens trounce 'em. Let's use the bathroom and watch some baseball, hopefully far away from those creeps."

"What's a 'rack,' Suze?"

"Well, Sis, you can have a rack of ribs or lamb, you hang clothes on a rack, and then there's a tennis rackette."

"But how did he know you had a 'nice rack'?" She wasn't buying my Bee Sting, so I resorted to distraction. It always worked when she was little.

"'How 'bout some peanuts or Cracker Jacks. I don't

care if I never go back,'" I sang as loud as I could as we exited King's and walked across the street to the Jack Ruhr Field where we saw the Mudhen's trounce the Red Wing Aces eight to four.

The distraction worked and we all enjoyed the game ... until the fight.

CHAPTER 11

The Fight

June, 1964

As I looked across the field, I saw the team walk out together to meet their families and girlfriends. Lots of high fives and laughter. No surprise since they were victorious Mudhens. I laughed just thinking about Mudhens all puffed up, strutting their stuff.

Hurry up, Eric. We'd have to cut this meeting short because the drizzle was fast becoming a shower. By this time most of the spectators were running to their cars, trying to avoid getting soaked. Maggie and Carrie had gone ahead to wait for me in the car since Carrie was exhausted and when she was exhausted she became Hyper Girl. Maybe we'd get lucky and she'd fall asleep in the car.

Eric looked around and I waved. He ran up to me and gave me a high five. "How'd you like your first Mudhens game?"

He was eager like a puppy ready for a walk, and what a handsome puppy he was. Suddenly I felt shy and little nauseated. More like fizzy. Thank goodness he couldn't see me blush. Then lightning lit up the sky.

"One Mississippi, Two Mississippi...." we said in unison, laughing after each Mississippi. Each Mississippi was a second, and in five Mississippis we'd hear thunder. Sure enough, bam! We laughed and the tension and awkwardness disappeared.

"Walk me to the car? We can talk on the way." The rain felt good on my face.

Your hair is getting frizzy Your hair is getting frizzy. You can kiss a good night kiss good-bye with that hair.

I was so happy I wasn't even listening to that crabby teacher voice inside.

"Sounds like a plan," he said as he took my hand. *Hand-holding is so romantic. He must really like you to ignore that hair.*

"You were . . ." I was about to say "wonderful" when I heard another crack of thunder and felt a drenching rain. From drizzle to deluge in just a few minutes. The dirt parking lot, a field in a former life, was fast becoming muddy. The mud sucked at my sandals.

Before I could finish my sentence and tell Eric about my sleaze encounter at King's, Ace, came from behind and yelled, "So babe's gotta a boyfriend! Dude, have ya balled her yet?"

It would have been a clever pun if someone other than Ace had said it.

Gillette's Cavalcade of Sports

On the air live from the Jack Ruhr Baseball Field in Miesville, Minnesota. It is Saturday Night Boxing sponsored by Gillette razors. To look sharp ... to feel sharp ... to be sssharp. Buy Gillette Razors for the shave that drives women wild.

Rainbow House

From Miesville is Eric, "Cutie Pie" Watson, weighing 175 pounds and wearing blue and white and his opponent from Red Wing is Ace, "the Sleaze" Stranger, weighing 220 pounds and wearing a red and white jersey.

Our referee tonight is Suzan Bailey.

I want a clean fight. No rabbit punches, no punches to the kidneys, no punches below the belt. In case of a knock down, go to your corner and wait for the count. When you hear the thunder clap, come out fighting.

Round One: Staring...

Cutie Pie got right in Ace's face and looked directly into the Sleaze's piggy eyes.

Ace threw an intense stare.

Eric staggered back, hurt from the Sleaze's beer and cigarette breath.

No one wanted to be the first to break eye contact.

It was close, but Ace, never blinking, won the round.

Round Two: Shoving.

Ace opened with a left push, having no impact on Eric whatsoever.

Eric responded with a hard shove to Ace's shoulder, causing him to stumble. Using his advantage, Eric attempted a major shove to the chest, but slipped in the mud, giving the Sleaze time to recover.

Dancing in the mud with fancy footwork, the Sleaze went in for the kill, but ended up falling on his ass in the mud, making Eric the clear winner of round two.

Round Three: Insults...

"Don't disrespect my girl, asshole."

"Don't call me an asshole, douche bag."

"Your mother's a slut."

"You're ma's friggin' ugly."

"My ma's dead."

Ace has no comeback. The round's clearly Eric's.

Round Four: Humiliation.

When Ace tried to get up, he slipped and fell again. Splat. He was covered in mud, his jersey stuck to his protruding beer belly.

With mud dripping from his face, chest, and body, the ref had no choice but to call the fight.

After only four rounds, the winner was: Eric "Cutie Pie" Watson.

And the crowd went wild!

Actually the crowd, that'd be me, started laughing. Eric joined in as we snorted and hooted our way back to the car. I felt great, like Karma slapped Ace in the face when I couldn't.

"Now that was some fight, if you can call it a fight when no one hits anyone else. Sorta like the question 'If a tree falls in a forest and no one is around to hear it, does it still make a sound?" I said, reaching for Eric's muddy hand. "And some game! You were great, by the way."

"In the fight or the game?"

"Yes," I said. "Two hits. In the game, that is. Only evil stares, shoves, and put downs in the fight. You have a great future..."

"In mud wrestling?" Eric said as he finished my thought.

"Right on."

When Carrie and Maggie saw us, all wet and muddy, they joined the Laugh-In.

"You guys look like Peggy Sue and Pickles after their mud baths," Carrie said. "I wanna go out and play in the puddles. Can I please?"

"No way, José," Maggie said.

"Why do the big kids always get all the fun?"

Another philosophical question, for sure.

"Eric, we have to get you home and Miss Carrie, *you* need to go to bed. Here, kids, some towels to help with the mess."

I looked at Eric, all muddy and wet, still handsome. Carrie was right: Big kids did have all the fun.

This was the best night of my life.

CHAPTER 12

The Aftermath

June, 1964

The next morning lying awake in bed listening to the birds serenading me, I floated off into fantasy land:

> *Romantic fantasy number one:*
>
> *It was a balmy summer night, warm, with no humidity, a good hair night. My loathsome freckles faded in the moonlight. My ears and feet looked their best. A smell of lilacs, no ...cherry blossoms, much more romantic, wafted in the breeze.*
>
> *It was a clear night so you could see the stars, lots of shooting stars. My lover and I made wishes while looking deeply into each other's eyes. No, make that Northern Lights lots of pinks, yellows, greens and blues. Nah, that's way weird, too much like Maggie's house, and I don't think the Northern Lights can be seen in Miesville anyway.*
>
> *I'm going back to the stars. No mosquitos, cats, dogs, pigs, chickens or goats to bother us, just fireflies lighting up the night.*

*Eric and I are on the front porch steps. He's holding my hand, no caressing my hand. Elvis is singing "Can't help falling in love with you" in the background. He, that'd be Eric not Elvis, though I wouldn't mind Elvis, leans in to kiss me ...*Don't kiss him. You had onions on your burger.

Crap, I can't even fantasize right.

* * *

"Suze, I'm going to need your help picking up branches and cleaning up the veggie stand. I'm heading out to check the garden. Be right back." Maggie yelled up the stairs. My inner critic and Maggie sure killed that buzz.

"Coming," I said as I crawled out of bed. When I glanced in the bathroom mirror I looked like all the pictures I'd ever seen of Medusa. Not a good look. I brushed my teeth a long time and then gargled with Listerine. Yuck, but at least I might have conquered onion breath.

By the time I got dressed, corralled my hair, and made my bed, Carrie was already up and blabbing in the kitchen and Maggie was back from the garden, looking a bit down. Maggie this, Maggie that, blah, blah, blah.

"Maggie, Berry's gone. Could the storm have blown her away like Toto? I've looked everywhere." She started to cry.

"Honey, as soon as Suze has something to eat, we'll all look for her. Eric will help when he gets here," Maggie said as she gave her a hug.

"No need for breakfast, I'm still full from supper. Let's go find the cat," I said, taking Carrie's hand. We looked in the barn, no Berry. We looked around the yard, no Berry. Just then Eric rounded the corner, holding a cat.

"Is this one of yours?"

"It's Berry! Where did you find her?" Carrie ran to retrieve her best friend. "I was scared something happened to you," she said, squeezing Berry. The cat swatted her.

"She was crying in the wheel barrow by the veggie stand. I think she's hungry."

"See, Carrie, she didn't blow away. Take her to the porch and feed her. She probably could use a nap after the storm last night."

I thought I heard Carrie grumble, "You're not the boss of me...," as she left.

"Man, that was some storm. The wind, the hail. Lots of branches down. Any other damage?"

"I just got up. You must have driven by the stand. How bad is it?" Just looking at Eric made my tummy get all flippy.

"Well, there is some standing water, but nothing serious. It's a good thing you rolled up the awning or the stand might have sailed off into the night. Are you planning to open this morning?"

"Don't know. Why don't you come in for something to eat and we can ask Maggie."

"Are we open for business?" I asked. Maggie was sitting at the table with her head in her hands.

"I've seen the garden." She looked up and I could see she'd been crying. "I don't think there's much to salvage. I haven't checked all the seedlings, but, on first look, the greens are gone, for sure. Hail's the worst."

"Can't you replant?"

"Sure, but it takes awhile; greens are planted in cool

76

weather, definitely not summer. I can put in another crop of greens this fall, but I'm mostly concerned about the tomatoes, peppers, beans and my cukes." At the mention of cukes, she broke into tears. "What about my pickles? I was planning to make lots of pickles."

It was weird seeing Maggie break down like that; she always seemed so strong and independent. Nothing fazed Aunt Maggie. *Go figure.*

"Don't give up yet. Let's check everything out," Eric said. So we all traipsed to the muddy garden to assess the damage. It was pretty bad. Some plants were beaten to the ground, others torn and broken from the hail. The wind had ripped the pole beans from their supports and the tomatoes from their cages.

"I'll check on the animals," Eric said. I looked at Eric and mouthed *Thanks.* Maggie and I walked back to the house.

"Why's Maggie crying?" Carrie said.

"She's sad that her garden is wrecked."

"Damn storm," Carrie said, scowling. Maggie stopped crying and laughed.

"Guess we'd better make a sign saying the stand will be closed indefinitely. I'm going to my room for awhile, kids, and try to figure out an alternative plan."

* * *

My romantic fantasy number two.

> *Tall, handsome, muscular, dimpled Eric came riding up our driveway on his chestnut stallion. The stallion reared, kicking his powerful front legs, but Eric was in control. He took one look at me with his intense brown eyes and he knew I needed him, wanted him.*

77

"How can I help?" he asked. "I'm here for you, my darling." And then did he break into song? Maybe ... "Do not forsake me oh, my darling."

Cowboys and High Noon. *Pathetic. He isn't even bare-chested. You can do better.*

* * *

And I did do better. Eric came out of the barn with a sign that said, "Storm destroyed garden. Stand closed indefinitely." Eric said he'd be back tomorrow to help. Then he left, not on a stallion, but on his Schwinn.

The next day, plants, along with encouraging notes, started to appear in the veggie stand: a variety of tomatoes, squash, beans, flowers of all kinds, peppers, herbs, lots of cukes, even eggplant!

Two days later, Eric and his dad came by with his truck, shovels, and a load of rich black soil that stunk slightly of manure. City Girl didn't mind the smell at all. Thanks to my hero, the community of Miesville brought Maggie's garden back to life.

Talk about an "Alternative Plan."

CHAPTER 13

The Date

June ,1964

I think I've died and gone to heaven. After helping out in the garden last week, Eric asked me on a date to go bowling. I've really missed it. That would be bowling not dating, since I've never been on a real date. *But you're about to, girl. Remember to let the guy win. That's what girls do.*

Bowling was a big thing in our family. Dad taught me how to bowl when I was a kid of about six, strong enough to carry a kiddie ball weighing about five or six pounds. Of course, I threw lots of gutter balls at first, but then I started to get a few pins now and then.

"Suze, don't look at the pins. Look at the spots on the alley."

That helped a lot. I practiced my four step delivery with an imaginary ball over and over in my room. I got many imaginary strikes and even picked up splits. I got my first custom fit ball when I was ten along with a pair of size five bowling shoes.

The more I practiced the better I got. With Dad's coaching, I became one of the best bowlers in our youth league. But that was with my bowling buddies, not with a boy I like.

Oh, no, don't get all girly-girl self-conscious because a boy might be watching. Have you forgotten everything I've tried to teach you?

Now for the real deal: a bowling date with Eric. Actually, I was a bit nervous, and my bitchy, bossy Inner Voice wasn't helping one bit. It was a test. Do I bowl my best or do I pretend to be a bad bowler and not damage his fragile male ego?

Eric picked me up late afternoon on Saturday after a busy day at the "veggie" stand. The veggies were growing well, after all the community help, but not quite ready for harvesting.

We were still selling out of our baked goods and floral arrangements, so I was feeling pumped about the successful day and my date. We were hitting King's for 'burgers and fries before heading to the Alley Cat Lanes in Hastings.

The Alley Cat had only six lanes with a seedy bar in back. According to Eric, it was a hangout for loser guys from Hastings, Cannon Falls, and Red Wing who loved to drink too much and hassle the waitresses.

The smell of stale beer, cigarette smoke, sweat and *eau de* bowling alley filled the air. The sound of the balls hitting the pins combined with the pin setting machines added even more percussion to the Rock 'n' Roll. While we waited to get a lane, we rented shoes and "shopped" for house balls. I found a green swirly twelve pound ball that almost fit my hand. Eric picked a sixteen pound black ball with nicks and gouges marring its surface. If a bowling ball could get acne, his would have had a severe case.

"Have you ever bowled before?" Eric asked as we carried our balls and shoes to the benches. Most of the lanes were being used by couples on dates like us. The bar at the back was filled with noisy guys drinking beer. They'd probably hit the lanes later, hopefully after we'd gone.

"Some. My folks like to bowl and we sometimes go as a family." *I get your strategy. Let him think you're a horrible bowler and then hit him with a 500 series. Cool.* "How about you?"

"Me and my buddies sometimes go during the winter, but I'm too busy to bowl in the summer. Do you wanna keep score?"

"Sure." We put our balls in the ball return rack. "You go first." Eric picked up his ball, wiped his hand on the dirty towel attached to the ball return, and made his approach. He was strong and threw a fast hook, but missed the king pin and left the 1-3-6-10 spare. Once again he threw it fast and it hooked past all the pins.

"Oops. Guess I need more practice."

"That's a tough spare to make. At least you missed on the right side." I got my ball, found my spot, hit my mark and got a good solid strike. *I see you haven't lost your touch, girl.*

"This might be a long night. Are you sure you haven't done a lot of bowling?"

I grinned.

After my double and his second open, I decided to come clean.

"Well, I do bowl a lot — two leagues actually. But I don't always bowl well. This might just be my lucky day." I ended up with a 560 series. The better I bowled, the worse Eric bowled, but he was a good sport about it. He ended up asking for my advice and I showed him a few tricks about picking up spares and showed him how to spot bowl. He started to improve and ended up with two games over 120. We had a good time. Eric paid and we walked to the parking lot.

It was a beautiful night: cool, clear with a beautiful half moon shining. We held hands and were just about to get into the car when I heard a familiar voice.

"How bad did she beat you?" Then Ace laughed. I could see the lighted end of his cigarette.

"Get in the car, Suze," Eric said as he opened the car door for me. He walked around to his side and came face to face with the Red Wing Bully. "I don't want any trouble. Just let me get in and we'll leave."

"Not gonna happen this time, Hot Shot." With that he sucker punched Eric and he was down for the count. "Now we're even." Then Ace strutted back into the bowling alley like he was the King Pin. I ran to check on Eric who had a bloody nose and a cut lip.

"Are you okay?"

"Does it look like I'm okay?"

"Sorry, dumb question." I pulled my used bowling socks from my purse and handed them to him.

"Your bowling socks? You gotta be kiddin' me. Don't you have a hanky?"

"Hanky smanky, these'll work just fine. You can't smell anyway, not with a bloody nose."

Then we both laughed. He wiped his nose with my sock and then stuck the "clean" one up his nostril. I giggled.

"What is it about trying to have a date with you?" Every time he talked the sock fluttered. He was like a little kid who knew his antics would get laughs.

"I attract the winners, can't you tell?"

"I can see that. Does that mean I'm a winner?" Sock flutter.

"Eric, you'll always be a winner to me. Can you still drive?

"I think so." Flutter. Flutter. By that time I was laughing uncontrollably.

"That cute, huh?"

"Let's get you back to Maggie's. She can check you out, and throw my socks in the wash. Now stop fluttering." I snuggled up to Eric and put my head on his shoulder. He turned on the radio and Elvis was singing, "Can't Help Falling in Love." At least I got that part of the fantasy right ...and the kiss, of course.

CHAPTER 14

Mom

June, 1964

The next week was a flurry of activity: working in the garden, scavenging in the barn and junk yard, baking, planning the Artsy-Fartsy Extravaganza for August. And then Mom phoned to ask if she could visit if we weren't too busy. What a hoot! We were always busy.

Before this summer, I had no idea how hard Maggie had to work to maintain her lifestyle. The animals were a job, running the house was a job, maintaining a huge garden and yard was a job and she was doing it all with just Eric's help. Sure Carrie and I helped as much as we could, but we added a lot to her work load because she washed our clothes and cooked our meals and lifted our spirits when needed.

Mom wrote cards and letters every week, but she didn't tell us much about how things were going with her and Dad. I think she really wanted to talk to Maggie more than us 'cause Maggie had gone through a divorce herself.

She was coming on Wednesday and planned on

staying overnight. This was all very strange and unexpected.

* * *

"Carrie, did you pick some flowers for your mom's room?"

"Do I have to give her my room? If I sleep in Suze's room, she'll keep me awake. She snores."

"There's always the porch. You did that before." Carrie frowned, probably remembering her night with Berry batting her face and making "stinkies."

"Your mom needs her privacy and besides it will be only one night."

"I don't snore. I purr gently just like Berry," I said, laughing. Carrie stuck out her tongue.

"Carrie, answer my question please," Maggie said.

"I'll do it right away. Can I have one of your cute bottles for a vase?"

"Sure, sweetie, but you'd better hurry. She'll be here soon. Are you girls excited to see her?" Before Maggie had even finished her question, Carrie was out the door and into the garden. "And she's off! How about you, Suze?"

"I guess." I hadn't really thought about Mom or Dad that much. The longer I stayed with Maggie, the more I thought of this as home. And these past few weeks, I had been thinking mostly of Eric and the sweet kiss we shared. It was my first kiss and I wanted to treasure it and lock it up in my memory, along with all our conversations, our laughs, and our friendship.

Mostly I was scared to see Mom, scared to know what Mom and Dad had decided. What would we do if they divorced? Would we stay in St. Coud? Where would

Dad live? Where would we live? Would they get remarried to someone new? Is this why she's visiting, to tell us they're splitting up? None of my friends had divorced parents so I couldn't talk to them. My mind was buzzing with questions, none of which I could answer.

I walked out the front door onto the porch, avoiding the pooping phoebe babies who just stuck their butts over the nest and let fly. Then I heard a car horn and saw clouds of dust. I was hoping it was Eric, but it was Mom ... and was Dad driving? Dad, what's he doing here? Now I *was* nervous.

Carrie ran from out back, holding a very wiggly Berry. "Daddy, Daddy, you're here, too." Dad gave her a quick hug and kiss, then started unloading luggage. Yup, luggage. One night, my ass. Maggie looked at me with bewilderment and concern. This must have been a surprise for Maggie, too.

"Look who I have, Mom! This is Berry, my kitty. I found her and Maggie says we can keep her." Carrie ran up to Mom who tried to hug her kid, but the kitty got in the way, hissed, scratched Carrie and Mom, then ran away. I wanted to join her. "Damn cat," Carrie said, looking at the long scratch on her arm.

"When did you start to swear?" Mom looked at her scratch. "I'm tempted to do the same. Never mind, sweetie, come give your mom a proper hug. You, too, Suze." After a long and somewhat awkward hug, Mom said, "Now, let's help Jake get this stuff inside."

"I'll bet you're wondering about all the luggage. Worried that your mom will stay the summer?" I was ...for sure. "No worries, girls, I'm headed to the Mayo Clinic in Rochester for a few tests. Jake will take me and stay until we know what the next step will be."

"I hate tests, especially spelling tests," Carrie said.

"No, honey, not those kinds of tests. I've been having some 'female' problems and my primary physician suggested further tests at the Mayo Clinic. Nothing to worry about. I'm looking forward to some time with my girls and a long weekend with my very sweet and supportive husband."

Was that Dad she's talking about?

I looked at Maggie and she winked, assuring me that everything with Mom and Dad would be okay. That was the good news. Mom having to go to the Mayo Clinic was the bad news. Even a wink from Maggie wouldn't make that go away.

"I wasn't sure how long I needed to stay in Rochester, so, you know me, the old Girl Scout, always prepared. I have to be there on Thursday around two to check in, but it's only a little over an hour's drive from here, so we'll have lots of time to catch up. Jake took Friday off so he could spend the long weekend with me. I thought we could have a little mini-vacation, check out the sights in Rochester."

"Jake, it's good to see you. It's been a while."

Dad gave Maggie a hug and said, "Thanks for having the girls and us. I think I'll just head upstairs with the luggage. Where did you put us?"

"I can show Daddy," Carrie said, taking Mom's suitcase with both hands. "You're staying in my room. You're going to love my garden room. I'm sleeping in Suze's room and she snores," Carrie said as she dragged the suitcase up the steps. "When we're done, we can go see the gardens and the animals. I helped with the baking and you should see all the treasures we've scavengered for our Artsy-Fartsy Sale in August. And

Peggy Sue likes bananas, and Pickles likes me, and Suze has a boyfriend who holds her hand and gets in fights at ballgames, and Maggie cried a whole bunch when the storm killed her plants, but the neighbors helped her replant with eggplants. I didn't know eggs grew on plants, did you? And her garden is all pretty now wanna go see it? Stomp your feet in case we run into that big ol' bull snake." We could hear Dad laughing all the way up the stairs.

"Does she ever stop to breathe?" Maggie asked, laughing.

"Nope, Motor-Mouth is pretty much non-stop." I took one look at Mom and started to cry. "I'm really worried about you."

"I know, honey." Mom gave me a real hug this time, like she meant it.

"We want to know everything," Maggie said, taking Mom's arm. "We have some rhubarb cake and iced tea with your name on it. We can talk while Carrie is helping Jake get settled. And from the sound of the tour she's planning, it should take awhile."

"Lovely. It's so good to be with my family again," Mom said, wiping her eyes.

Maggie looked determined, and I believed if anyone could get Mom to spill the beans, it would be Maggie. Now I had to find a way to gag Motor-Mouth.

CHAPTER 15

Mom and Mayo

June ,1964

For Mom's arrival supper, Maggie and I grilled chicken that had been marinated in Maggie's special marinade: a mixture of herbs, oil, vinegar, garlic, and a bit of honey. We made potato salad with the new potatoes, radishes, and green onions from the garden and hard-boiled eggs compliments of Mrs. Minniver and her "girls." Maggie added "doctored" canned baked beans and a we made a picnic in the backyard. Strawberry shortcake and whipped cream made for a delicious dessert.

Carrie was totally wound up and spent most of the evening running around with the animals and yelling "Watch me!"

Finally, Mom took her upstairs around nine for her bath while Dad and I helped Maggie with the dishes and clean-up. I could hear Carrie asking for another story and a glass of water; lil' sis was famous for stretching out her bedtime routine. Maggie and I settled in with a cup of tea, waiting for Mom to make her escape, hoping for a conversation without "Watch me!" Carrie demanding all the attention. After helping, Dad escaped, saying he wanted to read some murder mystery. He knew we needed some time alone with Mom.

"Whew! That kid can certainly stretch out bedtime, but I couldn't say 'no.' I've missed her."

"We understand, Emma."

I wanted to say "Speak for yourself, Maggie," but I didn't want to start an argument. Maybe Maggie understood, but I knew my sister's games. She could be a real stinker.

"Ladies, that was a delicious supper. I'm stuffed. Thank you."

Finally an adult conversation with Mom. I bypassed the small talk in case Carrie interrupted with more demands. "Okay, Mom, what's going on? We're all pretty worried."

"Do you have any alcohol in the house?" Now I was really worried 'cause Mom didn't drink.

"I think I have some gin somewhere. I'll check." Maggie came back with a dusty bottle of gin.

"This is a leftover from my marriage; I got custody of the gin. Does booze get old?"

"No, only love." Mom laughed. *Now what was that supposed to mean? I thought everything was okay with Mom and Dad.* "As for the booze, I think it's drinkable regardless of age. Do you have any orange juice? I can have an 'Orange Blossom.' Jake and I used to drink those in college." Now that's a Mom I didn't know about. I suspect that's just the tip of the iceberg. Maggie brought Mom her drink. After a few big swallows, she looked ready to talk.

"Girls, here's the deal. I've been having painful and very heavy periods for some time now and when I went for my yearly physical and pap smear, the doctor found some abnormalities. He suspects uterine fibroids and wants more tests. I am also anemic which is understandable considering the heavy periods. Depending on what the tests reveal, I may have a hysterectomy which means a week or so in the hospital. Jake thought we should get a second opinion, so here I am on my way to the Mayo Clinic. I'm just not sure what to expect, so I probably overpacked. Oh well."

"Are you nervous?" I asked, 'cause I was.

Mom shook her head. "Not so much nervous as scared. At least I know that if I have fibroids, I most likely don't have cancer. Fewer than one in a thousand fibroids are cancerous." *Typical Mom and her need for statistics.* "The tests will help ease my fears, I hope."

At the mention of cancer, both Maggie and I exchanged worried looks. My mind went immediately to Eric's Mom and her untimely death from cancer.

"Don't worry, sweetie, I'll be fine. I'm one strong and determined woman. I have so much to live for." She smiled at both of us.

"Mom, can you read me another story?" Carrie yelled down the steps. I wondered if she had overheard any of our conversation.

"See what I mean?"

* * *

In the middle of the night Carrie woke me up, crying. "Honey, what's wrong?"

"I had a bad dream about Mommy. What if she dies?" I reached to comfort her, but she pulled away. "I want Mommy."

She's going to the best hospital in the world and she

will get the best doctors. But she might have to have an operation."

"What's a hyster . . .?" *She did hear us. No wonder she's scared.*

"A hysterectomy. It's a big, scary word I know. Remember when Phyllis had her tonsils out?" Carrie nodded. "Well, Mom has to have something called fibroids removed from her tummy and once she does, she'll be well and back to her old self."

"Oh," Carrie said, yawning. *Thank God she isn't asking more questions.* "Now Mom has a big day ahead of her, so we should let her sleep. How about I tell you a story?" I patted my side of the bed.

"You're not the boss of me," Carrie said, ready to get all crabby, but she didn't get out of bed to go to Mom's room. Instead she snuggled up next to me. I fluffed up the pillows and got ready to create a story fit for a scared little girl.

"Once upon a time there was a little girl named Carrie who loved kitties, pigs, dogs, and chickens."

"Don't forget goats."

"Right ... and goats. She wanted to take home every animal she found, even snakes." Carrie giggled. "Carrie and her sister, Ugly Gertrude, (another giggle) lived on a little farm in a little town called Miesville which means 'village of mice,' a perfect place for Carrie and her sister to live."

"Her sister's name is 'Ugly Gertrude,'" Carrie reminded me.

"How could I possible forget," I said, making an ugly face.

"One day, while they were out picking berries, they met a . . ."

"A monkey."

"Okay a monkey. I was going to say a prickly, ickly dragon, but we can make it a prickly, ickly monkey."

"It's a mama monkey who is sick."

"Hey, Sis, whose story is this anyway?" *Not mine apparently.*

"The mama monkey has to go to the monkey hospital called Mayo and she might have to have an operation and have her histers, no I mean fibers, taken out. And the mama monkey has a family who is very worried."

"What happens next, Carrie?"

"She has the operation and isn't sick anymore, but she has to stay at the Mayo for a week. Her family is very happy now that she is well. The End."

With that Carrie turned over and was asleep in just a few minutes, leaving me wide awake to make up my own ending.

CHAPTER 16

Mom Update

July, 1964

"Suze, it's your dad on the phone," Maggie yelled out the back door.

"I'll be right in." I yelled back, putting down the hoe I was using to weed the garden. Eric and I were working side by side, talking only when we felt like it. I felt so relaxed and comfortable with him that I welcomed the silences. He understood my feelings about Mom: the good, the bad, and the ugly. "Be right back."

"Do you want me to come with you?"

"No, but thanks anyway." When I got into the kitchen, Maggie was nowhere to be seen. She either wanted to give me privacy or the news was so bad she didn't want to witness my meltdown. I could hear Maggie puttering around upstairs. Carrie was outside throwing a ball to the dogs, chasing the chickens, and laughing devilishly. This would be my time to talk with Dad privately.

"How's Mom?" I asked, skipping the small talk.

"She's in recovery. When I talked to the doctor, he said the surgery went well. The fibroids were both the size of walnuts. Apparently this isn't unusual for women

Emma's age. They removed her uterus, so the problems she's had should be solved. No more sibs for you, Suze."

I was quiet for a few minutes while I absorbed the news. "You okay, Suze?"

"Yeah, I'm just relieved, I guess," I said, wiping my nose on my dirty t-shirt. "I can certainly live without having more sibs. Carrie is more than enough. I'm just so relieved about Mom and you. We were all worried."

"I know you were, hon. This has been a worrisome summer for all of us. But you need to know that your mom and I are getting counseling and we're going to be just fine. And she has the finest doctors in the world." At that, I started blubbering again.

"So what's next, Dad?"

"She'll be in the hospital for a week or more. I have to get back to St. Cloud in a few days, so I'm wondering if you and Maggie could visit her a few times. We'll have to take it a day at a time for awhile. Maggie has already agreed to have her stay at Rainbow House until her doctor gives her the okay to come home to St. Cloud. She'll be unable to resume her household chores for awhile and I thought it would be best to have her closer to Rochester and the clinic."

I wasn't sure how I felt about having Mom at Rainbow House because Eric and I were getting closer all the time and I wasn't sure I wanted to share any of my feelings with Mom. Maggie, Eric, and I had plans for the rest of the summer including the Artsy-Fartsy sale in a few weeks. We had furniture to re-purpose, decorate, and paint. We had cards and watercolor paintings to make plus the Pickle Extravaganza when the cukes come in which should be soon. I wasn't sure I wanted to baby-sit Mom while she recovered from surgery. We needed everyone on board for the next few months. Mom might just slow us down.

"Suze, are you still there?"

"Sorry, Dad, just trying to process everything."

"I'll be visiting on weekends to help out with the animals and garden, and Emma, of course."

Great, now Dad will be here as well. So much for a few months here on our own. And to think I resisted coming here at all. Now I don't want to leave and I don't want to share our new "home" with Mom and Dad.

"Would you like to talk to Maggie again?"

"Yup. And see if you can't corral Carrie for me as well. It was good to talk to you, honey. I've missed you kids."

"Sure thing. See you soon. I'll be right back."

"Maggie, Dad wants to talk to you," I yelled up the stairs. Then I went to get Carrie who was chasing Mrs. Minniver in the front yard. Suddenly in mid-chase Mrs. Minniver changed directions and went for Carrie who squealed and ran up the steps to the front screen door. She stamped her feet, trying to scare off Mrs. Minniver.

"Dad's on the phone and wants to say 'hi,' if you can stop chasing poor Mrs. Minniver."

"Mrs. Minniver is mean. She wants to peck me on the legs. Damn chicken," Carrie said under her breath. I knew I shouldn't react, but I couldn't help smiling.

"Maybe if you stopped chasing her, she wouldn't want to peck you." Actually, I understood Mrs. Minniver perfectly. Carrie was a pest that sometimes deserved pecking.

When I went back to work in the garden, I was feeling cranky. I wanted to do my own thing without my parents interfering. This was my magical summer and I didn't want to share it with them. Period.

"Well, what's the news, Suze?" That was Eric's standard greeting, and I wasn't in the mood for him and his clever rhyme either.

"I don't want to talk about it."

"Just tell me if your Mom's okay and then I'll shut up."

"She's fine."

"Thanks. Now I'll shut up."

We worked in silence for the next hour and then I started to feel guilty for being crabby.

"I'm sorry, Eric, for being such a brat, but Mom will be recuperating here and Dad will be visiting on weekends. I feel like I'm being invaded by family."

Eric didn't say anything, but I knew he was thinking of his mom, and suddenly I felt selfish and ugly. "Sorry."

"Come here, Suze. I think you could use a hug.

I looked up to see Maggie smiling at the kitchen window.

CHAPTER 17

Hospital Visit

July, 1964

Mom had her surgery on Monday and on the advice of the head nurse we decided to postpone our visit until Thursday when she was feeling better. That meant we had to do our weekend baking on Monday, Tuesday, and Wednesday. The rhubarb was running out, so we switched from rhubarb to strawberries. We made strawberry jam with lemon and mint, strawberry muffins with pecans, and strawberry custard pies which were my favorites.

The veggies were beginning to produce, thanks to the community, so we started harvesting green beans, sugar snap peas, zucchini, and new potatoes and oh, the beautiful flowers: zinnias, daisies, marigolds, snapdragons, cone flowers, brown-eyed susans, sunflowers, all waiting to be arranged. Busy days.

Since the hospital wouldn't allow kids under nine to visit, Carrie had to stay home with Eric as her baby-sitter. She threw a major hissy fit when we told her she'd have to stay home, but Maggie told her she could bake Mom some cookies and send her a bouquet of flowers.

"Maggie, I want to make chocolate chip cookies 'cause they're Mom's favorite."

"Sure thing, sweetie," Maggie said as she gathered the ingredients: bowls, measuring cups and spoons and the all-important recipe card.

"I can do this all by myself. I can read, you know, and I've watched you bake and it looks easy. You and Suze can do other stuff while I bake." Carrie had taken Maggie's red checkered apron and put it on. I remembered trying on Mom's dresses when I was Carrie's age and almost tripping over the skirt. Maggie's apron was almost to Carrie's tennis shoes.

"Sis, let me make that shorter so you don't trip and hurt yourself." Carrie kindly consented to let me roll up the waistband and double the ties around her skinny waist.

"Okay, you can go now," Carrie said as she went to the counter and tried to reach the recipe.

"Would a chair help?" I said.

"I can do this myself," Carrie said as she slid one of the kitchen chairs to her work station. "Now go away."

"Remember to come and get me or Suze when it's time to put the cookies in and take them out. I don't want you to get burned. I'll be in the dining room writing. Just yell if you need anything."

"And I'll be reading."

Carrie was alone in the kitchen for only a few minutes when she yelled, "How much is a capital T?"

"A tablespoon. The big one," I yelled back.

"How much is a capital C?"

"A cup. Use the big one," Maggie yelled, rolling her eyes. We both started to giggle. Maggie motioned for us to sneak a peak into the kitchen. We tiptoed to the door and looked in to see Carrie covered from head to toe in flour. There was butter and a broken egg on the floor, and sugar spread all over the counter. The cats had discovered both the egg and the butter and were lapping them up.

"It's a disaster!" I whispered to Maggie.

"How are you doing, honey?" Maggie said, trying to keep from laughing.

"*Shoo*, cats," Carrie said as the cats hissed their response. "Maggie, could you come here a sec'? Just you, not Suze." Maggie left and I heard her gasp and then Carrie started to cry. "I wanted to do this myself."

"It takes awhile to learn how to cook, but your grandma taught me and I'm going to teach you, but first we need to clean this up and then we'll start over. How does that sound?"

"Okay," Carrie said as she wiped her nose on her sleeve. "Come here, you." Maggie put her arms around Carrie and just held her. "It will be fine, sweetie. This time I'll teach you how to read a recipe and we'll make the cookies together. Okay?"

"Okay. Can I still tell Mom I made them?"

"Sure, honey. Next time you'll know what to do."

"Thanks, Maggie. I love you."

"Me too, sweetie."

A couple of hours later I smelled the sweet success of Maggie and Carrie's Chocolate Chip Surprise cookies. The surprise was that Carrie added Rice Crispies, smushed up Corn Flakes, and dried cherries. Yes, and some gratitude. Shocker: She actually thanked Maggie.

"Wanna try some of my cookies, Suze? I added Rice Crispies, Corn Flakes and cherries as my surprise." Carrie brought out a plate with three cookies on it. "You can't have more than three because the rest are Mom's and Eric's."

"They look and smell delicious. Mom and Eric will love them," I said and they did.

* * *

Since I'd only been in a hospital once when I had pneumonia at age eight, I wasn't sure what to expect from the Mayo clinic. It was much bigger and more elaborate, with its complicated corridors and maze-like layout, than the St. Cloud Hospital, but the smells were the same: disinfectant and bad food.

My hospital memories were colored by my fears. I was scared to be away from home and my parents, scared of needles, and scared I was going to die because the nurses would say the rosary outside my room. St. Cloud Hospital was very Catholic, and I thought that if I died, I would go to hell because I wasn't Catholic. Presbyterians, like me, didn't have a chance.

Now I was visiting Mom in the hospital. No public displays of Catholicism, no needles, at least for me, and no rosary-praying nurses. But I was still scared.

"How are you feeling, Suze? Hospitals can be frightening and this place is huge!" If Maggie ever decided to be a mom, she'd be terrific because she intuitively knew how to comfort and assure us kids.

"Okay so far." We walked down hallways, following signs, looking for Mom's room. Finally we found it. The door was closed. There were no praying nurses outside her door, no needles that I could see, and no yucky hospital food I could smell. *You can do this, Suze.* I knocked.

"Come in." Mom was sitting up in bed wearing a pink

bed jacket, reading a magazine and sipping iced tea. Her hair was "done," she had applied a touch of lipstick, and she was looking her old self.

"Give your Mom a hug, but make it gentle. I'm still a bit sore."

"You look none the worse for wear, Sis," Maggie said, giving Mom a kiss on her forehead. "We come bearing Carrie gifts," Maggie said as she held up a tin of cookies and I held up the garden bouquet.

"She picked and arranged them herself."

"And how about the cookies?" Mom said with a grin. Then Maggie and I told of Carrie's cooking misadventures, including a vivid description of the kitchen.

"Stop, you two. My side is hurting from all this laughing." So that's why she was holding a pillow to her tummy.

"I can just hear her say, 'I want to do this myself!' and 'You're not the boss of me.'"

"How much longer do you have to stay here?" I was remembering my hospital stay and how eager I was to go home.

"The doctors are very pleased with my recovery, but won't discuss my escape until Monday. Apparently things can still go wrong, but I'm optimistic. This has gone so much better than I expected. Other than being sore, I'm feeling pretty good."

"What about Dad?"

"Jake will be here this coming weekend and staying at a nearby motel. After Monday I'll have a better idea of what's next. Actually, I'm looking forward to spending a few weeks with you. I've really missed my girls. And someone has a very important birthday." Mom looked at me and smiled. "We can celebrate your birthday together. I should be strong enough to help out and not be too much of a burden." Mom stifled a yawn. I suspected she was hurting more than she let on.

"Since being here, I have had time to think: about my life, about my marriage. Granted I've been on some strong meds, but I've made a decision and I think it's a good one for the family."

"Don't keep us in suspense, Sis." *Oh, no, she's going to divorce Dad.* My heart started to pound. And my stomach was doing flip-flops, not the good kind like when Eric kissed me.

"I'm going to go back to school. I don't know what I'll study, but I want to do something more with my life than clean and cook."

Whew! Dodged a bullet with that one. No divorce, at least not yet.

Then Mom yawned. I got it. The mention of school had the same effect on me. "Sorry about that. The nurse gave me a pain pill right before you got here and I think it's just kicking in. Better give me some of Carrie's cookies before I fall asleep." Another yawn. "I'm more tired than I thought. Must be the excitement of having visitors."

At that moment, the nurse entered the room and shooed us out.

Mom's parting words were, "Tell Carrie her cookies were nummy. Especially loved the cherries — cherries and chocolate. Doesn't get much better than that." Yawn. "Love you."

And she was off to La-La Land.

CHAPTER 18

Appropriate or Not

July, 1964

When we got back from visiting Mom, Carrie welcomed us with, "Did she like my cookies and flowers?" All the while jumping up and down. No "How's Mom?" or "When's Mom coming home?" Even a question about the Mayo Clinic would have indicated an interest in something other than herself. I wondered if I was that self-absorbed at her age. Probably.

"She loved them," Maggie said. "Especially the cherries." Maggie waved at Eric as he rounded the corner of the house, looking exhausted. Carrie could do that.

"Thanks, Eric, for helping out — again. Well kids, I've got work to do, so I'll leave you three to chat."

"I see you survived baby-sitting," I said with a grin.

"Barely. She's a very busy girl."

"Tell me about it."

Carrie came up to me and started pulling on my shirt to get my attention. "Eric and I watered the garden and I watered Eric and Pickles, but not the cats. They don't like water sprinkled on them, " Carrie said, giggling.

Carrie's hair and clothes were still a bit wet.

"That she did. Pickles liked it better than I did, but once I got over the shock of being squirted by a Squirt, it felt good. How was your mom?"

Carrie took off at the mention of Mom. "Get into some dry clothes," I yelled at Squirt and Berry as they ran into the house.

"She's doing much better than I expected. She looked good, like her old self. But the nurse had given her some pain meds before we got there and she was very tired. The visit didn't last as long as we'd hoped. The doctors will let her know Monday when she can come home. By home I mean here." Eric looked a little surprised at the news.

"How do you feel about that?"

"Not sure. We have so much to do around here with the veggie and flower stand, pickle canning, and preparing for the art sale that I don't how we can take care of Mom as well. And I was getting used to being here without her and Dad. I kinda like being independent, doing my own thing."

"Maybe she'll be able to help a bit," Eric said.

"Always the optimist," I said. "I appreciate that. I don't know what Maggie or I would do without you." Then I felt myself blush. "Any other excitement?"

"Actually, I have some bad news. I found one of the cats, the short-haired red one, behind the barn. It looked like a coyote or something got it. Carrie doesn't know. I thought I'd let you and Maggie handle the situation. Hope that's okay," Eric said, hanging his head.

I went over to him. "Come here, you," I said giving him a hug. "You've certainly had quite the day. Sorry about that. What did you do with Rudy?"

"I wrapped him in an old towel and put him in the barn where it's cooler."

"Thanks. I think I'd better tell Maggie right away so we can talk about how to break the news to Carrie. And bury poor Rudy."

"Maggie will know what to do and what to say," Eric said.

"I hope so, 'cause I don't have a clue. Carrie might go bonkers like she did when her gold fish died or she might blow it off. Hard to tell with that girl."

* * *

Maggie and I had a chance to talk privately while preparing supper. I was washing green beans and new potatoes while Maggie was making meat loaf. When I told her about Rudy, she got a bit teary-eyed.

"He was a good mouser, one of the best. Rudy wandered into the yard the first summer I was in the house. He looked pretty grim — a torn ear, skinny, and crabby. It took a lot of time and patience just to get near him, let alone touch him. Eventually canned tuna won him over. Unfortunately, outside cats don't live long lives.

When Emma and I were growing up, we had a similar cat, an unneutered tom, who looked just as scruffy. I remember asking Mom, your grandmother, how she knew he was a boy, and she explained, calling the testicles *'chibongas.'*"

"What a funny word," I said, just as Carrie entered the room.

"What's a funny word?" Carrie said.

"Honey, you need to wash up before supper and then you can help me shuck the corn."

"Shuck is a funny word. I think pickles is a funny

word, too." Carrie left the kitchen, reciting all the funny words she could think of: "Freckles, underwear, poop, fart..."

"We've got a few more minutes before Chatty Cathy returns. Tell me more about the cat."

"Well, we adopted the cat and Emma was totally enamored. She named the cat Willie and would take the cat for walks in the wagon. He slept with her and waited for her to return from school. Willie tolerated the rest of the family, but he loved your mom and when Willie was run over by a car, Emma grieved for weeks. Dad offered to get her another cat, but she wouldn't hear of it. Emma kept saying he was her 'heart cat.'" Maybe that's why Mom was so against having pets. She couldn't bear having her heart broken again.

Dinner was over, the dishes done, the counters and appliances wiped, leftovers put in the fridge and it was time. No excuses.

"Can I go outside and play with the dogs? I've helped." Carrie was restless like a pup who had to go outside to go potty.

"You certainly have, but Suze and I would like to talk to you first. Sit down, please."

Carrie groaned, "Do I have to?"

Maggie nodded.

"Hon, I have some bad news about Rudy. Eric found Rudy dead behind the barn. It seems a coyote got him. I'm sorry, sweetie. Rudy was a good kitty and we'll all miss him."

Carrie, with head down, was quiet for a few minutes like she was considering her options: Stay cool or blow. Then she looked up and said, "We need to have a funeral. I'll pick the flowers and say the prayers, Suze can dig the hole, Maggie can do the music. We'll send Rudy off to heaven just like we do for people." She wiped her eyes and went to the garden for flowers.

"Well, we've received our orders. I wasn't expecting that reaction. Were you?"

"Not really. I thought she might freak, but she didn't seem fazed at all. No questions about heaven. No comments about Rudy and his being a good cat. Nothing. Weird, but the kid is weird. We shouldn't be surprised. I suppose I should start digging. Where would you suggest we dig the grave? Preferably somewhere easy. I don't want this to take forever."

"How about behind the barn where Eric found him? The soil has been turned over and should be easy to dig."

"Right."

"Before you go, what music would you suggest? I don't have any idea what might be appropriate for a cat."

"How about we sing 'How much is that kitty in the casket?'" We broke out laughing. Not at all appropriate behavior for a funeral.

"Laughing like that at a funeral reminds me of Mom's graveside service at North Star Cemetery in St. Cloud. Everyone was all sad and then Emma spotted an epitaph that said 'Arthur Hole and Wife.'

She whispered to me, 'Only A-holes allowed' and we got the giggles. And I mean the serious giggles. The more we tried to suppress them, the more we snorted. Boy, did we get a stern look from the relatives."

"How old were you when your mom died?"

"I was fourteen and Emma was eighteen, just old

enough to know better."

I kept thinking of Eric and his mom and how it would feel to lose your mother as a teenager.

"Maybe we should think of a an epitaph for Rudy. How about 'He never met a mouse he didn't like.'"

"Or 'I thought I saw a Tweetie Bird.' or 'Suffering' Succotash.'" Then we really started to laugh.

"I always loved *Sylvester the Cat* cartoons." Just then Carrie returned with a ragtag bouquet of flowers.

"Have you finished your chores?" We looked guilty and ashamed because we were behaving inappropriately.

"I'm going right now to dig his grave."

"And I'm going to find some music."

"And I'm going to change clothes. You should too. We should all look appropriate for his funeral."

I didn't dare look at Maggie for fear I'd start laughing again, and that wouldn't be appropriate at all.

CHAPTER 19

The Funeral

July, 1964

"Dearly Beloved, we are gathered here because some damn coyote killed my cat. I hate him, but I liked Rudy sometimes, when he wasn't hissing at me or killing a mouse. I like Berry much better and I hope he doesn't die — ever. Now we all have to say 'The Pledge of Allegiance.' Put your hand over your heart, Suze."

"Sorry."

We dutifully followed Carrie's orders and respectfully recited the Pledge.

"Now everyone has to say something about Rudy. It doesn't have to be nice 'cause he wasn't always nice."

"He was a very clean cat. He washed himself regularly," I said.

"Rudy caught many mice, a few gophers, and a rabbit that I know of. He was a mighty hunter," Maggie said.

"He scratched," Carrie added.

"Now for some music. Maggie, that was your job."

I was very curious about Maggie's choice of music, but when she started to sing, I knew she had nailed it." Carrie's favorite show was *Mr. Ed* and Maggie just changed a few words for the occasion.

A Cat is a cat
Of course, of course
Unless the cat is a horse of course
Unless the cat is Rudy-the-Cat
Instead of Mr. Ed!

"Thank you, Maggie. That was beautiful."

Then Carrie lifted Rudy's body, all wrapped up in one of Maggie's old towels, unrolled the towel and dumped him into his grave. Maggie and I gasped.

"What's the matter? Did I do something wrong?" She looked like she might cry.

"Usually the body is treated gently and with respect," Maggie said.

"I just thought you might want the towel back. It's still pretty clean," Carrie said as she shook the towel out and handed it to Maggie. Then with great respect and a little gentleness, Carrie tossed half the bouquet onto Rudy.

"I'm saving the rest until Suze is done shoveling."

When I finished covering Rudy, she carefully placed the flowers on top of Rudy's grave.

"Let us pray." Carrie continued in her role as officiant. We bowed our heads. "God bless Rudy even though he scratched. Amen. Rudy, I'm drawing a picture of you tomorrow and I'll make a cross for your grave too, but I'm too tired to make it tonight. Good bye for now." And Carrie marched back to the house.

"Wow, that was some funeral. She was so matter of fact about it all. Maybe the questions about a heaven for animals will come later after she has had time to process what happened."

"I told you she was weird."

"I was all set to tell her about how in Norse mythology

there was a bridge that connected the gods with humans and animals. Then there was St. Francis who thought all creatures had souls and were part of his spiritual family."

"Nope, not interested. She returned the towel Rudy was wrapped in. She's obviously not very sentimental."

The next morning when I was working in the barn I heard Carrie talking to Rudy at the grave site about the picture she had drawn.

"I drew this picture of a rainbow, some flowers and a few mice for you. I don't know if you like rainbows or flowers, but I do. It reminds me of my favorite movie." And then Carrie sang in her sweet little girl voice, "Somewhere over the rainbow ...bluebirds fly...."

I wiped my eyes and continued mucking out the stalls.

CHAPTER 20

Mom's Arrival

July, 1964

"Girls, your mom's on the phone," Maggie yelled from the kitchen. Both Carrie and I were harvesting veggies for the weekend.

"Yay, it's Mom! I bet she's ready to come home to Maggie's," Carrie said as she threw another bunch of carrots into her basket. Then she dropped the basket and ran into the house.

"Sure, I'll take your produce into the kitchen along with mine, sure I'll wash your veggies and put them in the fridge, and thanks, Suze, for taking care of my responsibilities."

I trudged into the house, feeling sorry for myself because I had to do Carrie's chores along with mine and because my mother would soon be invading my territory and my summer. *Major bummer.*

I couldn't help but wonder how Mom would affect my relationship with Maggie. Maggie was less a Mom and more an older sister or a good friend, and I didn't want that to change. I could confide in Maggie in a way I couldn't with Mom. Girl stuff and all that.

And Eric. Would he still be my boyfriend if Mom was always around? With Maggie, he felt comfortable enough to hold my hand or give me a hug. I don't know if Mom would approve.

"Mom's coming home in two days and Daddy's bringing her! Yay! She wants to talk to you too, Suze."

After a rather brief conversation, I learned that Mom would be staying with us for at least two weeks because she needed to be close to Rochester for follow up doctors' appointments and she wanted to be here for my birthday celebration. The doctor said she should limit her physical activity and not lift anything over fifteen pounds. She could do light housework, but nothing too strenuous. Dad would be dropping her off and then returning on weekends to help with chores.

In other words, the best summer of my life would soon be over.

Enter Parents. Exit romance.

* * *

Dad dropped Mom off two days later. She looked pale and thin, but she had a huge smile on her face. We all rushed out to welcome her.

"I'm so happy to be out of the hospital. I wouldn't recommend it — unless you're sick, of course. No big hugs quite yet, just kitten hugs for now. But you'd better watch out. In a few days, I'll be giving big ol' bear hugs." Then Mom growled. Carrie and I both laughed, remembering how she used to scare us with her growly bear hugs.

"Berry gives good hugs most of the time. One time I thought he was going to hug me, but he scratched me instead. I think I squeezed too hard. I'll try not to squeeze you, Mommy." Carrie gently put her arms around Mom. "Was that kitteny enough?"

"It was perfect, honey."

Maggie and I gently welcomed Mom. Then I ran up to Dad and gave him a big ol' bear hug. "Thanks, Dad, for bringing Mom. Will we see you next weekend?"

"You bet. I understand there's going to be some major pickle action. Emma and I can certainly help with that while you and Maggie mind the veggie and flower stand. I seem to remember that a certain young lady turns 17 that weekend. Maggie tells me there's a nice supper club in Miesville, and she's agreed to make reservations for us — my treat. Your 'young man' is welcome to join us. Emma and I look forward to meeting him." He paused to look at Maggie's Rainbow House like it was the first time he'd really seen it.

"'Your young man.'" Motor Mouth blabbed. *No surprise there.* "Wait 'til I tell Eric that he's now 'your young man.'"

"Maggie certainly sings his praise." He stopped talking and just stared at me. "My little girl has grown into a beautiful young woman." Dad actually had tears in his eyes. I had never seen him this emotional.

Just then Pickles rounded the corner of the house and Carrie took off in hot pursuit.

"Wait, Daddy, don't go until you meet Pickles. She likes a good scratch behind her ears like this." Carrie demonstrated. Pickles waddled up to Dad and allowed him to give her a good scratch. Then she grunted with delight and sat on his foot.

"This summer has been good for you girls." Dad carefully removed his foot out from under Pickles's butt.

Carrie giggled. "Now it will be good for Emma. Come on, kids, give your old man a hug." Mom gave him a kiss and whispered something in his ear. He smiled and said, "I love you." I think they're on the mend.

Then Dad got into the car and drove away with all of us waving good-bye.

CHAPTER 21

Mom, the Artist

July, 1964

Carrie and I took Mom up to Carrie's garden room to get settled. I put away her clothes in Carrie's dresser and took her personal stuff to the bathroom. When I got back, Berry had jumped onto the bed.

"Do you need to lie down, Mommy? Berry sleeps with me sometimes, but he can sleep with you if he wants to. I'll share."

"Sounds like a good idea to me. I used to sleep with a kitty many years ago."

"Mommy, why do you look so sad?"

"I was remembering my kitty named Willie. We were the best of friends, but then he was hit by a car and died. It will be nice to sleep with a kitty again. Just for an hour or so. I'm more tired than I thought."

"Our cat Rudy was killed last week by a coyote and we gave him a funeral and I was the pray-er. Suze dug the grave and Maggie made the music."

"Sorry about Rudy, but it sounds like you gave him a lovely funeral."

"Rudy was a mighty hunter and he kept himself very clean."

"That's nice, honey." Mom yawned.

"I'll come get you when lunch is ready. Maggie's making vegetable soup and a salad," I said, trying to get Carrie to shut up and leave Mom alone.

"If you kids like it, I'll get Maggie's recipe."

"Maggie doesn't use a recipe like she does when she bakes. She uses 'garbage,' throws in whatever's in the fridge like old salad and stinky cheese. She's made it twice now and I really, really like it. Not like soup in a can." Carrie wrinkled her nose in disgust.

"Hmm ...'Garbage' Soup. I like the sound of that." Mom yawned again.

"Come on, Sis, it's time to let Mom get some shut eye." Carrie looked longingly at Mom.

"It's okay, sweetie, I'm just going to take a little snooze and then we can chat some more."

I took Carrie's hand and we went to check out the "garbage" soup.

"Mom's interested in your soup recipe." At the word "recipe," Maggie chuckled.

"The only time I use a recipe is for baking because you need to know proportions. Baking is really a science while, in my humble opinion, cooking is more of an art."

"Okay Miss Arty-Farty, how do I make 'garbage' vegetable soup?"

"I use a basic veggie stock made from simmering all the veggies left over in the fridge, even greens like lettuce and spinach, the 'garbage,' then add some herbs like parsley, basil, rosemary, thyme. And salt and pepper, of course. I let it simmer for a few hours, strain it (the pigs like the residue) and then add some cut up fresh veggies from the garden. Today's soup has onions, zucchini, green beans, corn, tomatoes, leftover boiled new potatoes, and carrots. Right at the end I add a little cream."

"It smells like the garden," Carrie said as she begged for a taste. Maggie dipped a spoon into the fragrant concoction and gave us both a taste.

"Nummy," we both said in unison.

"For our salad we're having wilted lettuce. And rhubarb pie for dessert."

"Yay, I love wilty lettuce with bacon, but I don't like rhubarb pie." She made her sourpuss face.

"How about some cookies for dessert?"

"Yay, cookies," Carrie said as she started her pogo stick imitation.

"Sweetie, why don't you get your crayons and some paper and make your mom a welcome home card?" Carrie skipped out to get her supplies.

"And Suze we're going to need some red and green leaf lettuce for the salad. I'll get the bacon started. When you get back, we can discuss this weekend's plans for the stand."

"Sure thing."

I dumped the lettuce into the colander in the sink, and went to the dining room where I kept my project notebook and returned to the kitchen ready for some serious planning action.

"Ladies, let the planning begin. Baked goods? We've just about depleted the strawberries and the rhubarb has gone to seed."

"Right, but we do have loads of zucchini and the tomatoes are ripening in great quantities. I think we bake with the cukes and can with the tomatoes. I make a mean spaghetti sauce with onions, peppers, and garlic. If the sauce doesn't sell, we'll be eating lots of spaghetti this winter."

"Then we bake our butts off tomorrow to get ready for Friday's sale. Maybe Mom will feel up to grating the zucchini."

"What will Mom feel up to?" Mom said as she walked into the kitchen. "Something smells awfully good. This must be the 'Garbage' Soup the girls have raved about." She walked to the soup kettle and took a taste using the same spoon Carrie and I used earlier. *What happened to my germaphobic mom?* She never would have let us share silverware at home.

"That it is. We were wondering if you might feel up to grating lots of zucchini for the bread, cake, and muffins we'll be making."

"I'll certainly try. Are you using Grandma's recipe?"

"Yup. Remember when she'd try to get us to eat vegetables by sneaking them into her cakes and cookies, especially her 'spice' cake. It was loaded with these thin strips of green zucchini peels and you'd carefully pick them out. It took you forever to eat a small piece."

"I'd forgotten about that. My only memory of eating disgusting green things was when she told us peas were candy," Maggie hooted. "I still hate peas."

When lunch was over, Mom went with us to the garden and started picking medium to large zucchinis. Carrie followed with the wheelbarrow.

"Hey, girls, take a look at this one!" Carrie and Mom held up a huge zuke that looked more like a zeppelin than a veggie.

"Careful, Mom, you're not supposed to lift anything heavy. Let me take it."

"No, I can do it," Carrie said as she wrestled the big vegetable into the wheelbarrow.

"A Hindenberg zuke!" Maggie said, laughing. "I didn't see that one when I harvested a couple of days ago. You turn your back on a zuke and that's what happens."

"What's a Hindenberg?" Carrie asked.

"It's a huge balloon airship that carried people a long time ago," I volunteered.

"Can I go up in one?"

"Nope, too dangerous. There is the Goodyear Blimp, though. A blimp is another word for the balloon airship. Maybe we could find a picture next time we go to the library," Maggie said.

"Blimp's a funny word. If I find another cat, I'm gonna name him Blimpie."

"You've given me an idea, Carrie," Emma said. "I'm going to carve this zucchini into something, maybe an animal. You know, make a picture on the skin. It will be a great display piece for the stand."

A carved zuke. I just couldn't picture it, but by the end of the afternoon I could. Mom first sketched the design on the zuke and then used her manicure tools and some small knives to carve the design. She had created an intricate design of the Rainbow House, the animals, the garden, Carrie and me, all on a zucchini. It was a work of art. Mom an artist and a zucchini the canvas? Who knew?

CHAPTER 22

The Guys

July 1964

Carrie was helping us harvest vegetables for tomorrow and somehow focused on the eggplants. She had collected several dark purple beauties and brought them to show Mom.

"Mommy, can you make something from these eggplants? They're pretty, but they taste yucky and they're mushy."

"Hmm, that's going to be a challenge. Maybe a hippo? Or an elephant? A penguin? or maybe an imaginary critter. You could write a story that goes with it. How does that sound?"

"I love penguins and how they waddle? Can you make a penguin, please?"

"A penguin it is." While Mom carved, Carrie wrote her story and we slaved away in the kitchen, baking for tomorrow's market. After about two hours Mom emerged from the dining room holding her creation: a deformed brown penguin with no wings and no feet.

"I couldn't get this one right. The zuke was so much

easier than this damn eggplant. The eggplant gets brown once it's cut into. This one needs to be tossed I'm afraid."

"Oh no, I think I could make something from that. Have you girls ever had stuffed eggplant?"

We gasped at the thought. Maggie had made stuffed peppers and stuffed zucchini, but a stuffed eggplant? No way.

"Just kidding. I couldn't bear to do any more cooking. Maybe the pigs will like it," Maggie said, throwing it in the slop bucket.

"Doubt it."

"No mushy eggplant for supper tonight," Carrie said, making a fake sad face.

The kitchen was stifflingly hot. I looked at Maggie, sweat dripping off her face, curls plastered to her face. She looked sunburned. I imagined I looked the same. We had managed to bake about ten loaves of bread and four dozen muffins despite the heat.

"How about I take us to King's for 'burgers, my treat. It's air-conditioned," Mom volunteered. "After you two shower, of course."

"Are you sure you're feeling up to it? You must be tired after murdering that eggplant," I said.

"Mommy didn't kill the eggplant, she just wrecked it," Carrie said, coming to Mom's defense.

"Let's go outside to cool off and talk about supper. It's much cooler out back. I'll bring the iced tea and Kool-Aid for the girls. Suze, you get the glasses. Meet you at the picnic table." I dropped off the glasses and scooted to the garden hose to wash my face and hands.

Just as we were having our cool drinks, Eric

rounded the house, carrying a cooler, with his dad close behind, carrying a covered dish with a loaf of bread resting on top. Pickles and Peggy Sue brought up the rear.

Maggie and I were certainly surprised to see them. The last time I saw Nick was when he helped us after the storm. I watched as Maggie tried to brush the damp hair from her face. Hmm ... normally she wouldn't have cared how she looked. Mom beamed and Carrie squealed.

"Yay, we don't have to eat mushy eggplant." Carrie ran to give Eric a hug and shake his dad's hand.

"Remember me, Carrie?"

"Yup. You brought the stinky dirt for Maggie's garden."

"That I did and from the looks of things, that 'stinky dirt' helped make this beautiful garden."

"I'll show you the eggplants," Carrie said, taking Nick's hand. "Maggie wanted to stuff an eggplant. Yuck."

Mom knew about Eric, but had yet to meet him. Now I was really nervous. I wanted her to like him.

Girl, you look a bit the worse for wear, but relax, your mom will like him and his dad just fine. It's too late to do anything about how you look anyway.

"That's some garden, Maggie. Beautiful. No wonder everyone wants to buy your vegetables." Maggie blushed at the compliment. "Eric and I thought you ladies would like some supper. You've certainly fed my boy many times. Now it's our turn. We knew you'd be busy baking for tomorrow and it's just too darn hot to spend any more time in the kitchen."

"Pops made his famous macaroni salad, one of our

family's favorites, and I made potato salad. I've got cold cuts and cheese in the cooler, so we can make sandwiches. Oops, I forgot the mayo and mustard."

"No problem. I'll get them," I said as I went into the kitchen. Eric followed.

When we got to the kitchen, Eric said, "Come here, you. I'd like a hug."

"Eric, I'm all hot and sweaty. How 'bout I owe you one."

"You look beautiful to me." *Come on, Suze, you can't refuse a hug after that.*

Just as I was about to give Eric a hug, Maggie walked in. "Sorry to interrupt, kids, but I offered to slice a few tomatoes to add to the feast. When you kids are done with the snuggles, could you please pick some leaf lettuce and a few cukes?" Now it was my turn to blush. Maggie went to get the bowl filled with ripe tomatoes, got a stack of paper plates and forks, a slicing knife, and left. I gave Eric a quick hug and kiss and we went to pick and wash the lettuce and the cukes.

"Suze, where's the mayo and mustard?" Mom said with a grin. Busted. I ran to get the condiments. When I got back, Eric and Mom were conversing comfortably, a good sign.

"I understand you carve vegetables, Mrs. Bailey," Eric said and Mom laughed.

"I carved a zucchini showing the Rainbow House and 'murdered' a perfectly good eggplant, trying to make a penguin," Mom said. "I'll get better after more practice."

"She's pretty good already. We're using the carved zuke in the veggie stand tomorrow. It's beautiful," Maggie said.

"Mommy tried making a penguin from an eggplant,

but it didn't have any wings or feet. I wrote a story about it. Do you want to hear it?" *Oh, no, not one of Carrie's stupid stories. How embarrassing.* She ran into the house to get her story.

"Everyone needs to be quiet. My teacher says that before anyone reads out loud." Carrie stood straight and tall as she read.

"At least she didn't make us recite the Pledge," I whispered to Eric.

"Poppy's Opration"

by Carrie Bailey

Once upon a time, there was a pengin named Poppy. Her mom had a opration to get her histers out.

She was very worried about her mom and cried a lot. But her mom got all better and started to do art, like carving vegetables.

Mom carved a pengin from a yucky, mushy eggplant that looked like Poppy, but eggplant Poppy had no wings, or feet , and everyone at school teesed her.

"Poppy can't fly! Poppy can't waddle! Poppy is dumb!" all the kids said. So Poppy went to the hospital and got fixed just like her mommy.

The doctor made her feet and wings from leftover feet and wings. Then she got out and went home. The kids sorta liked her after her opration and didn teese her any more..

The end

There was an awkward silence at first, but then Eric broke into applause and the rest of us followed. Carrie took a bow and said, "Did you like it?"

"We sure did, sweetie," Mom said as she gave her a big hug.

While Eric and I were cleaning up, I found Carrie's story written in her childish printing and filled with misspellings. I folded it and slipped it into my pocket, intending to give it to her later.

Mom and Carrie had already excused themselves to get ready for bed, leaving Maggie and Nick talking at the picnic table. I waved at Eric. We needed some privacy as well and decided on a short walk around the property.

"I think she's very strange, don't you?"

"Who? Your mom or Maggie? By the way, I liked your mom."

"You know exactly who I mean."

"Nah, Carrie's just a kid with a vivid imagination who hates eggplant. Can't say that I blame her."

"Thanks, Eric, for supper and everything else. You're the best."

I took his hand and we continued our walk.

CHAPTER 23

Pickles I

July 1964

"We've got to do something with all these cukes, girls and boys. Today's perfect weather for canning pickles. So let's get pickin' and picklin'. We'll need onions for tomorrow's bread and butter pickles, dill, and garlic for today's garlic dills."

"Don't forget the cukes," Carrie added.

"Thanks, sweetie. Sometimes the obvious escapes me. Once we gather our supplies, we'll set up a station inside for washing jars, lids and making the brine. And a station outside for washing cukes and peeling the garlic, all the really messy stuff."

"Remember to stamp your feet when you go into the garden. I saw that big ol' bull snake in the corn the other day," Eric said.

"If I see or hear any snakes I'm heading — no I'm running — to the house," Mom said. We stomped our way to the garden like overweight soldiers in a military parade.

Mom, Maggie, and Carrie went to pick cukes while Eric and I pulled onions, picked garlic and cut dill.

Maggie helped Mom and Carrie pick the right size cukes for the pickles. If possible, the cukes should be of a similar size for packing the jars.

In just under an hour we were armed with baskets of cukes and onions, bunches of dill and garlic. Just as we were leaving, we saw Carrie jump up, holding a wiggly, squirmy snake.

"Mommy, I found that big ol' bull snake. Can I keep him?"

Mommy screamed, dropped her basket and ran into the house.

"I don't think she likes you, Charlie," Carrie said as she dropped the snake back into the garden.

"Carrie, what were you thinking, scaring your mom like that? That wasn't a bull snake; they're much bigger. You caught a little ol' garden snake," Maggie said, laughing. "Let's go see if she's all right. We can get ready for washing the jars and lids. I'll make the brine and a cup of tea for your mom."

"Kids, we're going into the house to check on Emma and start sterilizing the jars and lids. I'll get the brine going. Why don't you start sorting and washing the cukes and peeling the garlic. Just make sure there's no dirt on the cukes. I'll bring out a big dishpan for the cukes once they're clean."

I followed Maggie and Carrie inside to get a clean tablecloth for the picnic table, a small scrub brush for the cukes, and a bowl for the garlic. When we got inside, Mom wasn't in the kitchen.

"Mommy, where are you? I let the little ol' garden snake go, so you don't have to be such a scaredy cat. I'm sorry I scared you."

"I'm in my room, Carrie, lying down with Berry. She's

been a real comfort for this 'scaredy cat,' I can tell you."
Carrie ran up the stairs to be with Mom.

"Never a dull moment with that girl," Maggie said, rolling her eyes. I wasn't sure if she was talking about her sister or her niece. "Emma was always scared of snakes. She was a Girl Scout, you know, and she would go to camp every summer. One year someone put a garter snake in her bed roll. She's been terrified of snakes ever since."

"I'm not too fond of them myself. Now Carrie, on the other hand, would have picked up that bull snake. She seems fearless with the animals. Remember the rats? Of course, she thought they were squirrels. I've seen her squeal with delight when Mrs. Minniver chases her or when Buddy Holly butts her with his head. Most kids would be scared by all these animals, but not Carrie. I wonder how she'll adjust when we go back to boring old St. Cloud."

I wondered how I'd adjust to boring old St. Cloud, but I knew I couldn't dwell on that because it was pickle time!

"Okay, ladies, I'm ready once again to face the world, this time without reptiles, please."

"Right. I've made us some tea and when we're done, we can start washing jars and lids. Why don't you relax with your tea while Suze and I carry the jars up from the basement."

Then the real work began: the pickle preparations. While Eric and I scrubbed and peeled outside, Maggie, Mom, and Carrie washed the jars and boiled the lids and bands. Maggie made the brine with a mixture of pickling salt, water, and white vinegar. Then Maggie submerged the jars in the canner of boiling water, sterilizing them. Everything had to be hot to guarantee sealing. We could only do seven quarts at a time.

When all that was done, Maggie called Eric and me into the kitchen to demonstrate the art of pickle packing. Since she planned to enter several jars into the Dakota County Fair, she packed several jars to perfection. Everything had to be just so: cukes lined up according to size, jars labeled with a two by three inch label with her name, county, product, processing time and method, and date the product was packed.

"Now kids, your packing doesn't have to be perfect, but do try your best. Ready to pack, picklers?"

"Possibly," I said.

"Primed," Eric said, getting into the alliteration.

"Can I have a popsicle?" Carrie asked. Everyone burst into laughter. "Why is everyone laughing?"

"Positively perplexing," Mom said.

"Puzzling," Eric said.

"I get it! Your words all start with P." Carrie paused, thinking. "Please. Can I have a purple popsicle."

"Perfect, Picklepuss, but we're all out of grape," Maggie said.

Maggie used the tongs to bring us the hot jars. We had to pack fast, three-four cloves of garlic, several heads of dill, a few peppercorns, and finally the cukes. Emma followed with the brine, using a ladle to fill the jars about half an inch from the top. Then with smaller tongs Maggie removed the sterilized lids and bands from a pot of boiling water and we screwed on the tops and bands and returned them to the canner for fifteen minutes. After the fifteen minutes were up, Maggie carefully removed the jars with the tongs and put them on the kitchen table to cool.

After an awkward first batch, we got the hang of our assembly-line pickle production and the subsequent batches went more smoothly.

When a seal had formed, the lids would pop. Carrie was our official POP counter. She had a pad of paper and pencil and when a lid would pop, she would make a mark. Any unsealed jars we had to eat.

A horrible job, but someone had to do it. Once the jars were cooled and popped, we finished them with their calico "hats" and ribbons. Maggie had made labels with her brand name, "Maggie's Garlic Dills," and a quick sketch of Pickles the Pig.

By the end of the afternoon, we had made four batches of garlic dills: twenty-five "popped" jars and three "unpopped."

We sent Eric home with two jars of unsealed pickles and we cleaned up the kitchen to get ready for the next day's bread and butter pickle adventures, hopefully without the help of reptiles.

"How long is the house gonna stink of vinegar?" Carrie asked.

"Until we're done making pickles," I said. "Duh."

"What's for supper?" Only Carrie would dare ask such a question after an afternoon of hot, messy pickle production.

"I thought we'd have pickled pork chops with pickle gravy, a pickle salad and mashed pickles with butter."

"EWW!"

"Actually, honey, I don't have a clue."

"Well, I do," Mom said. "How about King's? My treat."

CHAPTER 24

Pickles II

July 1964

The next day we tackled the bread and butters, which meant a different process altogether. After gathering the medium size cukes, Eric and I joined the others in the kitchen for the slicing of the cukes and onions. Easier said than done. The slices had to be similar in thickness, preferably thin, same with the onions. Once sliced and placed in big bowls, Maggie added salt and covered them with a clean dishtowel for about three hours. Supposedly, that helped with the crisping.

Since Carrie wasn't allowed to use the knives, she and Mom worked on making the labels and calico hats for the pint jars. Carrie had drawn the cutest pig on each label and used Maggie's water colors to wash over her ink drawing, with Mom's guidance of course. I was learning all sorts of things about both Mom and Carrie. It seemed Carrie got Mom and Maggie's artistic flare while I got their hair. *Lucky me.*

"I want to help make the brine, Maggie. Show me how." Maggie had collected the ingredients: cider vinegar, sugar, turmeric, mustard seeds, and celery seeds.

She showed Carrie how to measure the ingredients and then left her alone for just a few minutes to run upstairs. Eric and I were relaxing in the living room while Mom worked on the labels.

A few minutes left to her own devices and Carrie created a family memory that was repeated at every Thanksgiving and Christmas for years.

Turmeric is an unusual spice; it's yellow/orange and is used as a fabric dye as well as in cooking.

Carrie managed to spill an entire jar of turmeric.

"I-can-do-it-myself" Carrie got a dish towel, wet it and tried to clean it up.

The more Carrie tried to clean up the spill, the more yellow-orange she became. Her hands, her clothes, even her face were a sunny, orangey yellow, along with Maggie's scrubbed pine kitchen table top and white linoleum floor.

Actually Carrie was a beautiful shade and looked great with the kitchen's red walls and assessories. She looked like the offspring of Big Bird and a pumpkin. Even Berry, her constant companion and best friend ever, got into the act. Rolling on the spilled turmeric, Berry, usually a white cat with black spots, became a light ginger cat with black spots.

When Maggie came downstairs and went into the kitchen, all we heard was, "Holy shit!"

It was the first time I had ever heard Maggie swear and that, of course, added to the Carrie Canon of Catastrophes.

When Mom saw the orangey mess, she added to the chaos by grabbing Carrie by the arm and getting some of the turmeric on herself. My family was turning orange in front of my very eyes. By this time, the Tangerine Princess, was hysterical and ran outside with Berry, now a ginger cat, close behind.

"Wow! I didn't know that was even possible," Eric said, trying not to laugh as he surveyed my family and the kitchen.

"I'd better go after her," Mom said.

"No, let me. You shouldn't exert yourself. Besides you look almost as bad as the kitchen. I think I know where she is."

"At least take some soap and a few towels and washcloths, not white ones," Maggie said.

"I'll go to the store and pick up some more turmeric, so we can finish the pickles," Eric said.

"Make it a small jar," Maggie said with a smile.

Ever since our arrival at the Rainbow House, Carrie liked to hide out in the hay loft where we first went "scavenging" for treasures. She'd hide when she'd done something wrong or when she was sad or scared. So I headed for the barn and sure enough I could hear her crying. She was hugging Pickles in her pen and sobbing. Pickles was now decorated with orange handprints, a stenciling project gone bad.

"Come on, Sis, I have soap and some towels. Let's try to get you cleaned up, so we can finish making the pickles. Take off those wet, orange clothes and we'll get scrubbing."

I got a bucket of water using the hose outside and started to scrub her face and hands. "Close your eyes, Sis, so we don't get soap in them."

Even with some serious scrubbing, she still retained a yellow tinge. Maybe we could pass her off as jaundiced. Looking at me, she started to laugh.

"Suze, you're starting to be yellow like me. And Berry and Pickles are yellow too."

Sure enough the jaundiced look was contagious. Then we both started to laugh.

"If we look like this, Maggie and Mom must be yellow too!" The laughter continued to build like bubbles in a shaken pop can and when we exploded, we launched into a full on water fight. Carrie started it with a wimpy splash of yellow water.

"Come on, Sis, you can do better than that." I grabbed the bucket and dumped it over her head.

"No fair, Suze!"

Then Carrie ran to the hose, turned on the water, crimped the hose, building up the pressure and simply stared at me. "Now, I've got you."

I started to run, but Carrie unleashed the blast. While running away, I slipped in the muck and fell. Carrie laughed even harder, continuing to blast me until she eventually got tired holding the hose. Then she plopped down into the mud with the hose still running.

"Turn off the water. I admit defeat. You got me good."

"Sure did. Now you gotta take off your clothes too 'cause you're dirty and yellow." Unfortunately, she was right. I didn't want to add my dirty, muddy, yellow self to the kitchen mess. So I also stripped down to my underwear and toweled off as best I could.

"We best get back and see what we can do to help," I said as I wrapped a towel around me to cover up what I could.

"I don't want Eric to see me naked," Carrie whined.

"Here's another towel," I said as I put my arm around my crazy little sister.

"I liked our water fight, Suze."

"I liked it too, Sis."

"I wish that funny spice had been green. Then I could've looked like the bogeyman, or the green witch in *The Wizard of Oz.*"

"A noble goal, kid, a noble goal."

* * *

When we got to the house, Mom was vacuuming the floor, the table, anywhere there was powdered turmeric. Carrie's big mistake was getting the turmeric wet which was why it turned into a dye and stained most of my immediate family.

"Now what happened?" Mom asked when she saw we were wet and muddy in addition to yellow. "I can't deal with any more drama today."

"We just had a friendly little water fight. No big deal."

"Go change so you can help us finish these pickles."

"Yes, ma'am."

"Can I still be the POP counter? I promise to stay away from that awful yellow stuff."

"Deal. Now get dressed. We'll get your dirty clothes later. We really need to get these pickles done. I hope they turn out because they've been in the salt much longer than called for in the recipe."

"Where's Eric?" I asked.

"He went out to get more turmeric so we could finish the pickles."

"He must think we're all bonkers."

"Can't say I blame him."

Maggie was washing jars, lids, and rings, getting ready to put them in the canner for heating. Mom and Maggie were still a bit yellow, like us, but with repeated baths and showers we should be presentable in time for the weekend sales.

"What can I do to help?"

"You can rinse and drain the cukes and onions in the colander, then make the brine. The recipe is next to the ingredients, but you'll have to wait for Eric to add the turmeric."

"You called?" Eric slammed the screen door.

Carrie yelled, "Hooray."

"Well, ladies, you're looking a bit less yellow. There's hope for you yet." Eric set the turmeric and three frozen Chef Boy-ar-dee cheese pizzas on the counter. "I figured we could add some stuff and we'd have supper."

"I've always wanted to try these, Eric. Thanks."

I made the brine, got it boiling, added the drained cukes and onions and turned off the heat.

Maggie brought the hot jars to the kitchen table and we packed the pickles, added the brine to one half inch from the top, and then sealed them. We added the packed jars to the water bath for fifteen minutes. Then we began to count pops.

We had enough pickles left to make a few more jars, but we were all pickled out by that time. We were hot, sticky, and yellow, but we had seven pint jars of bread and butter pickles. The cuke mixture that we didn't can, we put in jars for refrigerator pickles.

"Why do they call them bread and butter pickles anyway?" Eric asked.

"I was curious about that myself, so I checked it out in the library. These pickles were popular during the Depression when meat was scarce, but cukes and onions weren't. Apparently they were used in sandwiches instead of luncheon meat."

"Could we put them on the frozen pizza?"

"Nah, but we can add onions and peppers to the pizza. That would be good."

"And more cheese, maybe some olives ... anyone else getting hungry?"

"Why don't you guys go outside to relax and Suze and I will make supper," Eric said, giving me a wink.

"Susie and Eric sittin' in a tree-ee — K-I-S-S—I-N-G," Carrie sang.

"Outside. That means you, too, Squirt," I told her.

CHAPTER 25

The Talk

July 1964

That night I had trouble sleeping; my brain was in overdrive, thinking of tomorrow's market, plans with Eric and the family, Dad's visit, my birthday. Plus I was hot. Sleeping with Carrie was like curling up next to a space heater on a hot, humid day. She was thrashing about, kicking me in the back. So I went downstairs, hoping to sleep on Maggie's very uncomfortable couch. And much to my surprise I saw a light on in the kitchen and Mom having a cup of tea at the kitchen table.

"Hey, Mom. What are you doing down here? Too hot?"

"Yup. I just couldn't sleep. How about you? Too excited about your birthday?"

"Nah, Carrie's a hot wiggle worm and she kept kicking me."

"Tell me about it."

"Usually there's a breeze, but not tonight. Mind if I join you?" That sounded weird and oddly formal, even to me. She's my mom, after all, why would she mind, but it's been awhile since we had a private talk and we were definitely outta practice. Usually, Motor Mouth, a.k.a. Squirt, dominated every conversation. I took a cup from the dish drainer and poured myself a cuppa from Mom's teapot.

"I've been wanting to talk to you alone for quite awhile, especially now that you have a boyfriend."

Oh, no, The Talk, a moment I've been dreading since I got my period back in 6th grade.

"Mom, I know all about the 'birds and the bees.'"

"I know you do, honey, but do you know about heartbreak and despair?"

I did not want to have this talk.

"Let me tell you about my first love." she continued. "They stick like glue, you know. Considering your sister's pickling adventure, maybe a better comparison might be they stain you like spilled turmeric on a kid's t-shirt."

"Let me guess: It wasn't Dad."

"No, it wasn't. I was in high school about your age, seventeen, when I started dating Matthew, funny, smart, handsome, Matthew who wanted to become a lawyer. The only other guy I had dated was a mindless jock who only wanted to make-out."

Did Mom actually say 'make-out'?

"Matthew and I continued dating through our senior year and promised to stay together through college. We were naive and in love. Mom had died that spring and I was very vulnerable. I wanted to be with someone safe and steady. Matthew was all that and more."

"What happened?" I was really getting into this talk. I had no idea about Mom's romantic past.

"We both went off to school — me to business school in St. Cloud and Matthew to the University of

Minnesota. Then my whole life changed: Dec. 7, 1941, Pearl Harbor Day. Almost six months to the day after graduation we were at war. Matthew enlisted the spring of 1942 and after basic training was sent to North Africa. We wrote often during basic, but after he shipped out there were only two letters and the phone call from his parents. There were 479 killed and he was one of them. The funeral was one of the saddest things I'd ever experienced."

"Oh, Mom, that's terrible. You lost your mom and then Matthew, too, in only two years. How did you cope?"

"Not very well, I'm afraid. I was still living at home, trying to help the family. Dad was grieving Mom's death and drinking quite a bit, so he wasn't emotionally available for me or Maggie. Maggie was the one who got me through it. We went to movies, read books together, talked. I guess I needed to share that with you because our young men might be going to war too, a war that I fear will escalate. I worry about you and Eric. So no, honey, this is not 'the talk' about sex, but about the impact of first loves. I've never really gotten over Matthew's death. The ghosts come out at night."

"Tell me about Dad," I said, wanting to continue the mom/daughter bonding. "Why wasn't Dad drafted?"

"He was, but he was turned down because of his poor eyesight. I was very grateful."

"Did you fall in love with Dad right away?"

"Another time, sweetie, I'm exhausted. It was good talking with you — as a friend. I've missed you."

"Me too. Sleep tight, Mom."

"Don't let the bedbugs bite." Mom finished the rhyme. "Or the ghosts keep you awake." Then she kissed the top of my head and went upstairs.

I took my tea to the front porch where it was much cooler. I sat in one of the rockers with Berry on my lap until the sky lightened, displaying colors that rivaled the Rainbow House.

Please, Eric, don't ever go off to war.

CHAPTER 26

The Birthday

July 1964

When Eric arrived that morning to help out with the veggie stand, I couldn't wait to see him. Talking with Mom about Matthew's death got me thinking about Eric and me. He'd graduate in a year and could actually be drafted. We needed to talk.

"Eric, you're finally here!" I ran up to him and gave him a big hug and kiss.

"Wow! That was some welcome. What did I do to deserve that? What's going on?"

"We can talk later if you can hang around awhile. Let's just say I'm glad to see you."

"Isn't this your birthday weekend?" Eric flashed me a grin. "I have a surprise for you."

"My, aren't you mysterious? When do I get my surprise?"

"Maybe tonight? I'd like to take you to King's after you close the stand."

"I can't. Dad's coming tonight and Maggie's making a special supper."

"Bummer."

"You're coming to Wiederholdt's on Sunday. Right? Maggie's made the reservations for four o'clock 'cause Dad needs to drive back to St. Cloud. Personally, I'd rather go to King's, but my parents want to try the hotsy-totsy 'supper club.' Since they're paying, I can't object. Have you eaten there?"

"Yah, it's good. I like their barbecued ribs and hash browns."

"We're coming back here for birthday cake and ice cream. Maybe after that?"

"Deal. Now we need to get to work."

* * *

Eric and I harvested the veggies while Mom and Carrie made bouquets and Maggie loaded baked goods into the wagon. Mom carefully placed her zucchini art in the center of the stand, and surrounded it with baskets of fresh vegetables. Maggie included a recipe card for each basket of tomatoes, zukes, etc. featuring that vegetable. We didn't include recipes for our baked goods because that would be like "shooting ourselves in the foot," to quote Eric.

We made a sign that said, "Maggie's Dills and Bread and Butters ready next week!" Once everything was artistically arranged by Mom and Maggie, Eric returned to the barn to see to the animals. We were open for business.

Our first customer was Mrs. Hotsy Totsy herself, an attractive woman about Mom's age, a confident business woman who was wearing a print sleeveless shirtwaist and sensible shoes.

"Good morning, Mrs. Wiederholt. What can we do for you today?" Maggie was polite and efficient in her greeting, not overly friendly, but not cold either.

"I'd like to talk to the artist who carved the zucchini."

"That would be me," Mom said shyly.

"How much would you charge for something like that?" She pointed to the carved zucchini.

"I'm not sure. I'll have to think about it and get back to you."

"The club, that would be Wiederholdt's—" She forced a smile that missed her eyes, "—is hosting a groom's dinner next Friday, and a sculpture such as this would be unique. Could you do something wedding appropriate? I'll pay you well. Oh, by the way, Maggie, we'd like lots of your flowers. Small bouquets for the twenty tables and something more showy for the buffet table. Bright, happy colors. Could you manage that?"

Both Mom and Maggie stood there with their mouths open.

"We could," Maggie said, once she regained her composure.

"Price everything out and bring the invoice to the club on Sunday. I understand you've reservations for six to celebrate someone's birthday." I gave her a little wave. "Happy birthday, young lady. We do include a complimentary birthday cake that can be shared. See you then." She marched back to her Buick and drove away.

"What just happened?" I said to Mom and Maggie, who were still in shock.

"I think I just got my first commission," Mom said.

"Me too. And I don't have to bake Suze a cake."

* * *

Once again our baked goods were a smashing success. We sold out by Saturday which meant we canceled the market for Sunday, my birthday. That meant the "girls" could sleep in, which meant we were up and at 'em by nine, awakened by the smell of bacon and coffee. Dad had done the morning animal chores and had started breakfast.

We cleared off the dining room table, used some of the flowers left over from the market as a centerpiece and set the table with Maggie's best dishes. Dad made blueberry pancakes with diced-up bananas and strawberries and fried the bacon crisp and crunchy, just as we liked it.

"Thanks, Jake, for doing this. It smells divine."

"A birthday breakfast for the birthday girl."

"Thanks, Dad."

"Here's to Jake." We all held up our orange juice glasses to toast the chef.

"And to the birthday girl. To Suze and her Sevententh!"

"I understand, Emma, you are now a recognized artist," Dad said with a twinkle in his eye. "A wedding zucchini sculpture. Who knew a vegetable could become a work of art? I guess that means I'll be a bachelor for another week."

"Poor baby," Mom said as she patted Dad's hand. "I have my final doctor's appointment on Wednesday and they should clear me to go home next weekend. I'm excited to register for school this fall. I'm thinking of art as a major."

"No need to rush into declaring a major. Take your time. Try a variety of classes," Maggie said.

"So, Emma, what are you thinking of carving on your zucchini?" Dad laughed. "A bride and groom perhaps?"

"I've talked with Mrs. Wiederholdt about the couple

and I found out some helpful details. The groom is taking over his father's pig farm and his wife plays the piano and teaches music. I think I can work with that."

"I think you should have Pickles and Mrs. Minniver looking in the church window."

"That's a fine idea, Carrie. All the farm animals could be peeking in the church windows to see the ceremony. I could make the sidewalk leading up to the church look like sheet music with lots of flowers on both sides of the walk. I'll get sketching tonight." I looked at Dad and he was trying hard not to laugh at the thought of pigs and chickens on a zucchini.

It was pretty funny, but Mom was serious about her commission. It would be the first time in their marriage that she had earned any money of her own.

"Close your eyes, Suze, we have a surprise for you." Mom and Dad went into the kitchen and came back with a box wrapped in colorful birthday paper.

I opened it to find a brand new Polaroid Camera. "Wow! I love it. Thank you so much."

"Honey, you'll also find a couple of rolls of film, to get you started." I ran over to both of them and gave them big hugs, bear hugs, not kitten hugs. "Be sure to read the instructions and be a little careful with taking pictures; the film's expensive."

"Yes, Dad, I will."

"Well, since people are giving gifts, Carrie, why don't you get your gift and I'll get mine." Carrie ran, giggling all the way up and down the stairs, and Maggie went to the kitchen and brought back a small package.

"Me first! Me first!" Carrie yelled, handing me her present.

"Hold your horses, Sis."

148

"Hurry up."

"I'm trying, but did you have to use a whole roll of Scotch tape on this?" I said as I finally got the wrapping off.

"Carrie, this is beautiful." I took out a watercolor painting of Eric, Pickles, Berry and me in the garden. "Did Maggie help you?"

"Well, a little, but I did most of it. Do you see the snake? I drew that as a joke 'cause snakes are easy to draw and Mom's scared of 'em. Maggie helped me frame it. Do you like it?"

"No, Carrie ... I love it!"

"Yay, she loves it!"

"Now open mine," Maggie said as she handed me a small package wrapped in yellow tissue paper tied with a red ribbon. I opened the small box and inside was a gold ring with a red stone.

"Maggie, this is beautiful."

"So that's where Mom's garnet ring went. When I went through Mom's jewelry case after the funeral, I couldn't find it. So what's the story, Maggie? Why did Mom give you the ring? I always suspected she liked you better." Mom smiled at Maggie.

"And I always thought she liked *you* better."

"Mommy, do you like me or Suze better?"

"Hush, sweetie, I love both of you to bits. I want to hear Maggie's story about the ring."

"Right before she died, she gave me the ring to keep for her first born granddaughter. I'm not sure why she gave it to me, not you. Maybe she figured I'd be the first to have a baby."

"Well, she did catch you making-out a few times." Mom smiled.

"That she did. I honestly don't know why she gave it to me, but she made me promise. After spending so much time with Suze this summer, I decided this would be the perfect time."

"You're right. This is the perfect time. Thanks for keeping it safe."

I tried on my grandmother's ring and it fit. "Thanks, Maggie, Mom, and Grandma. This has been the best birthday ever."

"And you haven't even gotten Eric's present yet," Carrie said, as she made kissy-kissy noises. "I don't care if I don't get a ring 'cause I don't wear jewelry anyway. So there."

"Well, I have little surprise just for you, Carrie. When your mom was at the Mayo clinic, they were advertising sheets of commemorative stamps celebrating their 100th anniversary. I bought a sheet of stamps for you at the post office. Someday they'll be worth a lot."

"Worth more than Grandma's ring?"

"Possibly. You could be sitting on a small fortune."

"Yay, me!"

CHAPTER 27

The Dinner

July 1964

"Do I have to wear this ugly dress? I hate my hair in braids. Stop, you're pulling. What if I spill on the tablecloth? Will Mrs. Wiederstuff get mad at me and not want to buy Mom's zucchini or Maggie's flowers?" Carrie was freaking out and we weren't even there yet. I had to agree with her that her yellow dress was ugly and a bit too small. Besides she was still a bit yellow herself.

Then there was my dress. We'd each brought only one "dress-up" outfit and mine wasn't a favorite either. The summer I'd planned was one where dress-up meant a clean t-shirt. Instead, I was wearing an old-lady shirtwaist, just like Mom, only mine was shorter and didn't have a belt. I couldn't be old at seventeen, could I? I tried my hair down with a ribbon head band and it looked pretty good, considering my curls. Not exactly like Jackie Kennedy, but I was trying. Today wasn't too humid so I hoped it would stay that way.

Mom insisted we dress like we're going someplace fancy. If we'd been going to King's like I wanted because it was my birthday, we could dress in t-shirts and shorts. When I thought about it I supposed it was a celebration for all of us: Mom and Maggie because of their commissions, Dad because he and Mom were going to stay married, and me because it was my birthday. And what was Carrie celebrating?

"I hate these ribbons. Why can't I let my hair down like Maggie? I wanna be like Maggie," Carrie whined. I figured it out: Carrie was celebrating being the world's biggest brat.

"Ready, girls? Eric's here," Dad yelled up the steps. Dad looked like he usually did going to work. Black dress pants. white shirt only without the tie and suit jacket. His dark brown, short hair was neatly combed, his black horned rim glasses clean, his freshly polished black wing tips shiny. He reminded me of an old Buddy Holly. Speaking of Buddy Holly, our Buddy Holly had gone AWOL. We hadn't seen him for several days.

Eric was spiffed up too and looked equally uncomfortable. Dressed in ironed khakis and a blue dress shirt with rolled up sleeves, he was holding something behind his back.

"Hi," I said, suddenly feeling awkward and shy.

"You look nice," Eric said, blushing. *That's something you two share. You can be embarrassed together, how sweet.*

"So do you."

"Happy Birthday. I brought you something." He held out a wrist corsage, my very first, made of carnations, roses, and baby's breath — a corsage from an actual florist. "And a small one for you, too, Squirt."

"I got one, too! Yay me!" Carrie gave Eric a big hug. "Can I sit next to you when we get there? Carrie got a camera for her birthday, and a picture from me, and a ring from Maggie. What did you get her?"

"It's a secret, Squirt,"

"See? A new camera." I held up the Polaroid for everyone to see. "And I'll be taking pictures of all of you, so it's a good thing you've dressed up. Yes, Dad, I read the instructions."

"Well, kids, think we can all squeeze into the Buick? Carrie, you sit between me and Mom; Maggie, you get the back seat with Eric and Suze." Wiederholdt's was about a ten minute drive from Maggie's. I hoped we'd have enough conversation to last.

"Did you know that Wiederholdt's used to be a grocery store, a tavern and a gas station? Just three years ago they made it into a restaurant," Eric said from the back seat.

"What's the difference between a bar and a tavern?" Mom asked.

"Not sure, but I think a tavern serves food as well as alcohol. I think tavern sounds classier than bar," Maggie said.

"Wouldn't that make King's a tavern?" I asked, showing my preference for King's.

"Without the class," Maggie said, laughing. We were both remembering our encounter with Ace and his gang.

"I think bars and taverns are essentially the same thing. They both serve liquor," Dad said.

"My teacher says that when two words mean almost the same thing, they're cinnammons."

"Synonyms, Carrie," I said, correcting her. She turned around and gave me one of her looks that said, "Buzz off, Sister." Then Dad turned on the radio.

"Thank goodness," I whispered to Maggie.

"Well, we're here," Dad said, as he pulled into the crowded parking lot. "Time to celebrate!"

Mrs. Wiederholdt, the hostess-with-the-mostest, met us at the door with menus for all. "I hope you've brought the invoice with you, Maggie."

"That I have." Maggie handed her an envelope.

"We can talk business after you have your dinner. I'll show you to your table. Ethel will be your server. Enjoy your meal."

"Remember I get to sit next to you, Eric."

"Aren't I lucky to be between two lovely ladies?" Eric pulled out our chairs.

After a tasty dinner and excellent birthday cake, we were just getting ready to leave when Mrs. Wiederholdt asked Maggie to come to her office.

"Why is Maggie going with Mrs. Wiederstuff?" I started to correct Carrie, but she gave me that "Buzz off" look again.

"Probably she wanted to discuss the terms of their consignment. I hope she doesn't think their prices are too high and cancel the order," I said.

"I don't think that will be the case, sweetie. Maggie and Emma would underestimate their value not inflate it. I worry about people taking advantage of them. I saw how low you priced your produce and baked goods."

After about ten minutes she returned, grinning.

"You'll never believe this," Maggie said. "She wants to buy a lot of my produce along with the flowers through October. The cooks want to use more produce actually grown in the area, to cut costs and add quality. One of our cooks is a regular customer of mine, so she knows the quality of our veggies. They will give me a list of what they want a few times a week. What I can't provide, they'll get elsewhere."

"Is she still okay with the zucchini art?" I could tell Mom was concerned that she had changed her mind.

"More than okay, Emma. She added $10 dollars to your price."

"Wow, I'd better get going on that. If I make a mess of it, I can always start over with a new zucchini, right?"

"Just don't try anything with the eggplants," Maggie said, with a smile.

"On a practical note, won't the orders from Wiederholdt's make a lot of extra work for you?" Dad, always the practical one, asked a very good question.

"I've got Eric." Maggie looked at Eric and grinned.

"I can use the extra hours, saving for college, school clothes, car expenses."

"And I've got the girls for another few weeks. We'll be busy, that's for sure, especially with the Artsy-Fartsy sale coming up, but we'll manage. We have so far. Once the pickles are ready, I'll try to sell those as well. The ones on the relish tray were good, but not fantastic like ours."

When we got home, Eric and I stayed on the porch to have some private time. Dad was packing, getting ready to return to St. Cloud for the work week. He'd be back on Friday to help with chores and then he and Mom would go home, finally. Eric and I were just getting comfortable without all the family around when we heard Carrie yell.

"Buddy Holly, you stay away from my corsage. Suze, help me!" Carrie rounded the corner with Buddy Holly and Berry in hot pursuit. Berry ran in front of her and she tripped, falling face first into the grass. Her outstretched arm made the corsage very available to Buddy Holly.

"Carrie, are you okay?"

"Damn goat!" Carrie said as she got up and brushed off her ugly yellow dress. "Here, you've already eaten the roses. You might as well have the whole thing." Carrie took off the remains of the corsage and threw it at Buddy Holly. He happily nibbled away, eating the entire thing, even the ribbons.

"Now, where's my camera?"

CHAPTER 28

The Gift

July 1964

"Let's go for a ride maybe get some ice cream. You can't have birthday cake without ice cream, right?"

"I'll let Mom and Maggie know we're taking off for a few hours and say good-bye to Dad. Be right back." By the time I got back, Carrie had claimed Eric and was bending his ear. He needed rescuing.

"Come on, Eric. I've checked in and checked out."

"Where ya goin'?" Carrie looked at Eric and I shook my head. *Please don't tell her, Eric.*

"Just for a little ride. I want some private time to give Suze her birthday present. You should stay here to make sure your Dad gets all packed and ready to go home. I'll be back tomorrow and we can chat. See ya."

Carrie looked a bit crestfallen, but she quickly got over it when she saw Mom and Dad come out on the front porch with Dad's luggage.

Eric waved and said, "Thanks again, Mr. Bailey, for the ribs. See ya next weekend."

"Bye, Dad, drive safely." I lowered my voice. "Let's hurry so we don't have one of those long Minnesota good-byes. I hate those."

"Me, too."

We got into Eric's Chevy truck and took off to Cannon Falls for ice cream, at least that's what I thought we were going to do, but instead we went to Lake Byllesby.

As we drove up the road to the beach and picnic area, I was astonished by the size of the lake compared to Lake George, the puddle of a lake close to my high school. Lake George was pretty, though, and allowed us a nice skating rink in the winter, but that's it. Sometimes kids in the neighborhood caught a few perch or sunnies. Nothing like this.

Families were having picnics, kids were splashing in the water, a few fishermen were trolling, and a speed boat was pulling a water skier attempting to slalom ski.

I've always loved lakes and hoped that we would someday own a cabin on a lake. Not likely to happen.

"This lake is huge!"

"Byllesby is over 1300 acres and is fifty feet deep in places. Dad and I fish here once in a while. Mom loved it here."

"Tell me about her, if it isn't too hard." Eric took a blanket from the truck and we found a spot in the shade and got settled.

"Would you rather sit on a bench?"

"No, this is fine. I'd like to know about her."

"She was fun, funny, and 'full of beans' as Dad used to say. And a great cook! I think that's one of the main reasons I appreciate Maggie so much. Mom was also teaching me to cook because she knew that I would need to be able to take care of myself. When I think of Mom, I smile and remember all the fun we had as a family. After she got sick, she tried to make everything okay, normal, you know? But it never was the same. And Dad was a mess, stretched to the limit with his work, the medical bills, and Mom. I tried to help, but I couldn't do much. I'd read to her after school and she tried to help me with my homework, but she'd get so tired." Eric started to cry.

I put my arms around him and let him cry. We sat there for some time until he'd cried himself out.

"Happy Birthday, Suze," he said and we both laughed. "This wasn't what I'd planned at all."

"Me either. I wanted to talk about what you're going to do after high school. Mom and I had a chat in the middle of the night when we couldn't sleep because of the heat and our hyperactive brains. She told me about her 'first' love, a guy she dated in high school. He was killed in the war a year after they graduated. She also said, first loves 'stick like glue' or 'stain like turmeric on Carrie's t-shirt.' I don't want that to happen to us."

And then *I* started to cry.

"Don't we make quite the pair, crying our eyes out on your birthday?" Eric said, giving me a great big ol' bear hug.

"Promise me, Eric, you won't enlist."

"Promise. How about we dry our eyes and I give you your gift?" He pulled a small jewelry box from his pocket. "Here. I hope you like it."

I opened the box to find a gold locket on a dainty gold chain.

"Oh, Eric, it's beautiful. I love it." Then I gave him a big ol' kiss. "Help me put this on." He kneeled behind me, lifted my hair from my neck and gently fastened the clasp. It felt cold and warm at the same time. Then he kissed my neck and I melted. I wasn't sure what I was feeling, but it was intense and it made me slightly uncomfortable. "Umm, Eric, I think we'd better go before we end up 'making-out.' Can you believe my mother actually said that she dated a dumb jock who only wanted to make out all the time?"

Eric, got up and pulled me to my feet. Then he shook and folded the blanket. The awkward moment was over.

"Yeah, it's always a shock to see your parents as real people, teenagers even. Boy, did I get the stories from Dad about his teenage years."

"Your Dad was probably about draft age when the war started. Why didn't he go overseas?"

"Mom and Dad were living in Red Wing at the time where he was teaching, and his job was considered important, so he was exempt from the draft. Plus he was married and Mom was pregnant with my brother."

"I didn't know you had a brother."

"I don't. Christopher lived for only a few hours. He had a heart defect, so I never knew him, but Mom talked about him a lot right before she died."

"Why does life have to be so sad?"

"Cause that's life, I guess. Come on, Suze, we need ice cream. There's a neat soft serve place in Cannon Falls called The Dairy Inn. How about it? Please tell me you didn't bring your camera."

"Yup, it's in the car. I can hardly wait to see you with ice cream on your face, and when you least expect it, 'surprise, you're on *Candid Camera.*'"

When I was getting ready for bed that night, I took off the locket and put it in my dresser drawer. I was scared of losing it and wanted to keep it safe, like Maggie did with Grandma's ring.

As I was reliving my day before falling asleep, I realized that the locket wasn't the gift; Eric was.

CHAPTER 29

The Prize

July 1964

It was Monday and nobody liked this particular Monday. We were all tired and low energy after our busy weekend. Plus, it was raining and we still had to do chores.

Maggie and I were in the barn dealing with the animals. Mom was on her third zucchini, trying to get the wedding scene just perfect for Friday's groom's dinner. Carrie was playing in the rain with Pickles and Peggy Sue and having a ball. She could have fun whenever and wherever, rain or no rain.

"This will be a good day for taking it easy," Maggie said. For Maggie "taking it easy" meant cooking or canning, washing, drying, and folding clothes, doing her art projects, getting ready for the Artsy-Fartsy sale next month, or writing a story, essay, or poem. My idea for "taking it easy" was taking a nap.

Maggie had invited Eric and Nick for supper. She planned to make fresh tomato spaghetti sauce which had become a favorite of ours. She sauteed onions, peppers, and garlic before adding lots of fresh tomatoes, basil, and parsley from the garden. Then a dollop of honey, her secret ingredient. She said that balanced off the acidity in the tomatoes. Who knew? She'd let the sauce simmer to thicken. Served over pasta and topped with some grated cheese, it was delicious.

A salad with her homemade dressing, Eric's surprise pie for dessert and you've got yourself an inexpensive feast. Gotta love a boy who can bake and an aunt who can cook.

"Hey, anybody home?"

"In the kitchen," I yelled.

"I brought in your mail," Eric said as he pushed open the front screen door. Berry brushed up against him, purring. The other cats couldn't be bothered. "At least you're happy to see me." He bent down to scratch her behind her ears. "Something smells mighty good."

"Ha, caught you talking to yourself," I said, touching my necklace.

"I was talking to the cat," Eric said. "Can't give you a hug 'cause of the pie and the mail."

"How 'bout I take the pie and the mail," I said, setting both on the kitchen table. "Now we can have a proper hug."

"Me, too," Carrie said.

"Sure thing, Squirt."

"Me, three," Maggie said, wiping her wet hands on her apron. "Where's Nick?"

"He'll be here shortly. He wanted to clean up before dinner."

Maggie picked up the mail and sifted through the ads, the bills, and then tore open an envelope and let out a big squeal.

"I did it!" Maggie squealed in delight again.

"What's all the noise about?" Mom came down the

back stairs after her nap. She was getting stronger every day, but still needed to rest a lot.

"I won a poetry contest for *McCall's* magazine. I can't believe it," Maggie said, waving the check.

"Are you rich?" Carrie wanted to know.

"Not unless you call $50 and a year of free magazines rich," Maggie said, still laughing.

"I didn't realize you wrote poetry. I thought you were mostly interested in short stories and essays. Way to go, Sis," Mom said, giving Maggie a big ol' bear hug. She must be feeling much less sore. "All right, let's hear the poem."

"I knocked, but you guys were making so much noise, you didn't hear." A freshly-shaved Nick came into the kitchen looking neat in a clean shirt and jeans. "What's all the excitement about?"

"Maggie's a rich and famous poem writer," Carrie said. I didn't bother telling her the word was *poet* because I didn't want "the look."

"Maggie was just about to read her poem, Dad." Eric grinned. " She's going to be published in *McCall's* magazine."

"Wow, a poet in our midst! Impressive. So let's hear all about it."

"I hope I can remember how it goes." Maggie brushed the curls off her face, wiped her hands again on her apron and recited:

Weather Report

Old lady fog lifted her skirt,
shook the moisture from its folds,
plucked a hanky from her sleeve
and sneezed a rainbow.

When she heard the word "rainbow," Carrie started to jump up and down, her signature move. "I love rainbows."

"Hmm, I will never look at a sneeze or mucus the same way again," Nick said, flashing Maggie a dimpled grin.

Mom wrinkled her nose. "I love how you made the weather an old lady because that's what it feels like sometimes — a crabby old lady. Two dollars a word, too, a pretty good return for your efforts."

Leave it to Mom to count words.

"Good thing I brought a bottle of wine, so we can toast Maggie's success." Nick held up a bottle with wickerwork around the bottom.

"I hope you brought a corkscrew," I said.

"I've got one here somewhere." Maggie rummaged through several drawers.

"Found it. Suze, would you please get the wine glasses?"

"You have wine glasses? Who knew?"

"Oh, shoot, they must all be broken."

"You've never had any wine glasses. Admit it."

"Busted, but these will work. Right?" Maggie held up her mismatched juice glasses.

"They're perfect," Nick said as he struggled with the corkscrew. "Hope this is okay. I told the liquor store clerk we wanted something for spaghetti. He suggested this *Chianti.* I thought the bottle was pretty neat." Nick poured the three adults a small glass of red wine each. "To Maggie and 'Old lady fog.'"

Mom gave Carrie and me a taste. "Gross," Carrie said and I agreed. Eric refused even a taste, but the adults seemed to enjoy it. The dinner, the dessert, the cheerful conversation made for another perfect family gathering.

When I went to walk Eric to his truck, I reached up to give him a good night kiss and he looked at me funny.

"Eric, is something wrong?"

"Suze, where's your necklace?"

"I had it when I met you in the kitchen because I remember touching it."

"Okay, did you leave the kitchen or dining room any time tonight?"

"No, I don't think so. I did use the downstairs bathroom, but other than that — no."

"Let's go back in and look. I remember seeing it at dinner and thinking how nice it looked on you."

"Oh, Eric, I feel terrible." He took my hand as we walked back into the house.

"We'll find it, I'm sure." Eric and I looked high and low in the kitchen, dining room, and downstairs bathroom. No necklace.

Mom and Carrie had gone up to bed and Maggie and Nick were sitting at the picnic table outside, so they were no help.

"Suze, I'll be over tomorrow morning and we can retrace our steps to my truck. It's useless to search in the dark. If it's outside we'll find it in the morning. Don't worry." He gently kissed me good-bye.

I went upstairs to get ready for bed, heartbroken that I'd lost that beautiful necklace. Thank goodness, Carrie was sleeping with Mom tonight. I wanted to be alone.

When I took off my blouse, about to unhook my

bra, I saw the necklace nestled between my breasts.

Relieved, I finished washing my face and brushing my teeth, my usual routine, and then went downstairs to use the phone.

"Eric, it's me. I found the necklace."

"Fantastic. Where?"

"In my bra."

We both started to laugh.

"Ace was right. You do have a nice rack."

CHAPTER 30

The Picnic

July 1964

We all went to Rochester with Mom for her doctor's appointment because Maggie and Mom wanted Carrie to see the famous Mayo Clinic. Dad had given her the commemorative stamps and they thought she'd be interested. *Wrong:*

Size of the campus. "Are we there yet?"

The Mayo Brothers' statues. "Who are they again?"

The subway tunnel shops. "I wanna go outside."

Carrie couldn't care less about the quality of the medical care because she was totally focused on our picnic and swimming plans.

After Mom's checkup, we had agreed to meet Eric and Nick at the Lake Byllesby beach and picnic grounds for supper. We had all brought our swimsuits, lawn darts, and a cooler filled with goodies. We had agreed it was time for a family outing before Mom had to go home. We just had one more weekend all together.

"Are we there yet?" Carrie kept asking from the back seat. I could tell the kid really needed to get out of the car and exercise. A good paddle would be just what she needed.

One of the good things about living in Minnesota with so many lakes, ten thousand to be exact, was that most kids were taught how to swim at a young age.

Mom and Dad insisted that we both take swimming lessons. I had completed Junior Life-Saving and Carrie had finished the Beginners' class and would have gone to Intermediate classes if we had stayed in St. Cloud for the summer. We could both swim reasonably well, at least in a pool, which is definitely not the same as lake swimming.

"Won't be long now," Maggie said. She was really patient with Carrie's incessant questions and blathering, while I was tempted to gag her with whatever was handy, which would have been the towels in the back seat.

"Wow, that's a big lake!" Mom said as we pulled up to the parking lot by the picnic tables. She turned around and looked directly at Carrie, "Now, Carrie, remember what we talked about. No swimming without an adult present and you must stay in the shallow area. Do you understand?"

"Are Suze and Eric adults?"

"Good question, honey. They're getting close." Maggie laughed. "Now I'm going to need some help getting all this stuff out. Let's find a table in the shade." We all helped Maggie unload, Mom being careful not to lift anything heavy.

"I have to go to the bathroom," Carrie said. "Then I can change into my suit."

"Of course you do," I said through gritted teeth. Carrie always waited until the last minute to go to the bathroom.

Before we left the clinic an hour ago, we all went, but,

of course, she didn't have to go … then. *Typical.* She was waiting until we got to the lake.

"I'll take you and change, too," I said as we walked to the public bathrooms.

"It's kinda stinky and wet in here."

"I'll try to find the cleanest stall for you to change in, but be sure to go potty before you put your suit on. Okay?"

"You keep guard so no one comes in."

Carrie did as requested and came out in her pink flowered one piece.

"My turn. You stay here, Carrie, and keep guard while I change. Then we can go wading in the water." By the time I finished changing into my white one-piece, Carrie was gone.

I walked to our picnic table and was surprised to find no one there. Looking out toward the water, I saw Mom holding up her skirt and wading with Carrie. Maggie, wearing a short skirt and blouse, was laughing and splashing them. Nobody seemed to care if they got wet. Good thing 'cause I was ready to join in the fun.

"Hey, guys, wait for me." I ran in the warm sand straight into water up to my knees, splashing the "girls." Then I walked further and further into the lake until it was deep enough to actually swim and I did a quick crawl to the floating raft and back. It felt wonderful.

Carrie was showing Mom and Maggie how she could do the crawl, but it was more like thrashing about than swimming. It didn't make any difference to the "adults" who thought she was an "exceptional swimmer for her age." She was "exceptional" all right, but it wasn't because of her swimming.

After about an hour of goofing around in the water,

we got out, dried off, and got the food ready for the guys. Sure enough, they were right on time. Eric had come from the Rainbow House after doing the chores and then picked up his dad. Both exited the truck in shorts and tees. I looked over at Maggie and she was grinning from ear to ear. So was I.

Carrie had persuaded Eric to play lawn darts. We played it all the time at home. You put the two plastic yellow rings at a fair distance apart. Carrie was still little so about twenty to twenty-five feet apart would be fair for her. Each player got two darts. Each time you threw the dart in the ring you got a point. They had sharp points, but darts were weighted so they would stick in the ground. They played while we got things ready. Nick was wading in the water, cooling off before supper.

The next thing we knew people were pointing and yelling about some kid who went beyond the ropes. The kid seemed to be struggling. Nick saw the problem and quickly swam to where the kid was and got there before he went under again.

Maggie saw the whole thing, but Mom and I were oblivious until the noise became too loud to ignore. Nick swam back in good lifesaving form and basically saved the kid's life.

Once he got the boy onshore, his mother was all over her son for disobeying her strict orders to stay within the ropes. He coughed a few times and then his mother dragged him by the ear to their picnic table.

Nick just shook his head and laughed. The crowd applauded and Nick bowed.

What we didn't know was that someone had taken a picture of Nick's carrying the boy from the water and turned it into the Cannon Falls local newspaper, the

Beacon. He laughed it off, but Maggie and Eric were awfully proud.

Good Samaritan Saves Boy

by Connie Johnson, staff reporte*r*

On July 25th at Lake Byllesby Beach an unidentified man, wading in the water, saw seven year old Matt Schmidt, screaming just beyond the ropes indicating deep water. Without hesitation the man swam to young Matt and pulled him back to shore where his mother admonished him for disobeying her orders.

"I wanted to see if I could swim to the raft," Matt, the son of Arline and Butch Schmidt, said in a recent interview. "I did, but I couldn't swim back."

"I told him not to and he deliberately disobeyed my orders. His father and I have punished him accordingly. He has been banned from the beach for the remaining summer. Just the kiddy pool in the back yard for him. We would like to thank the Good Samaritan for rescuing our boy."

Upon learning the man's identity, the Schmidts sent Nick Watson a beautiful bouquet of flowers from Arline's Flowers for All Occasions located on Main Street.

When the excitement had died down and Nick had dried off, we had our supper of chicken salad sandwiches, potato chips, veggies and dip, watermelon, sugar cookies, pop and iced tea. Clean-up was a breeze because we ate out of the containers and threw away the paper plates.

"See, Carrie, what can happen if you get in water over your head," Mom said, trying to scare Carrie into being very careful. "That little boy thought he could swim much better than he could and he nearly drowned. It's a good thing Nick was there to rescue him."

"I bet I could have swummed, swammed ... I could've made it back," Carrie said, "'cause I'm an 'xcptional swimmer for my age.' You said so."

"You are, but lakes can be dangerous, sweetie."

"Sorry to be a party-pooper, ladies, but we have to go. Tomorrow will be a busy day and we have to get up early. I took the day off so Eric and I could check out a few college campuses. We're seeing both Mankato and Winona State Colleges tomorrow. Then in a few weeks or so we'll head north to St. Cloud, Duluth and Bemidji."

"Will you be back in time to help this Friday?"

"Sure thing, Maggie," Eric said, giving her a hug. "Thanks for the supper. It was great."

"I'll walk you to the truck," I said, taking Eric's hand.

Nick walked over to Maggie and kissed her gently on the cheek. Then he squeezed her hand good-bye.

"You were very brave, Mr. Nick," Carrie said, giving Nick a hug.

"My turn, Squirt," Eric said as he hugged me.

Please, please, Eric, pick St. Cloud State.

CHAPTER 31

The Box

July 1964

"Come on, Carrie, we're going scavenging again," I yelled up the steps. "Maggie and I are headed for the barn to search for treasures. Hurry up!"

"I'm going potty. Can't you wait a few minutes?"

"You know where we'll be."

Maggie and I left for the barn. It wasn't too long before Carrie showed up, with toilet paper stuck to the bottom of her shoe.

"I just made a new kitty toy. If I stick toilet paper on the bottom of my shoe with soap and water, then Berry chases it."

Leave it to my sister to capitalize on an embarrassing moment.

"Are you ready to scavenge?"

"You betcha!"

"I'm bringing Berry." Clever Carrie had taken an old towel and made a sling around her neck and put Berry in it so she could climb the ladder using both hands. When she got almost to the top, Berry wiggled his way free and scooted to the hay bales in search of critters. We each went our separate ways and started to search.

After going through two cardboard boxes of receipts, bank statements, and paperwork that should have been tossed years ago, I finally hit "pay dirt." It was a wooden box, about fourteen inches by twelve inches, carved with the initials L.M.J. The box looked handmade with dovetailed corners. It was quite beautiful.

"Maggie, look at this. What kind of wood do you think this is?"

"My guess is pine, a common wood and easy to work with. Have you opened it?"

"It has a lock on it. I didn't want to force it."

"Let's take it into the house. Years ago I bought a canning jar filled with old keys at a garage sale, intending to make something with the keys. Good intentions, the story of my life. I remember there were some small ones in the jar. I think it's still in the basement."

"Oh goody, a treasure chest. Maybe we'll all be rich," Carrie said. "Berry, you stay up here and catch mice. We'll be back in a jiffy."

Maggie found the old jar in the basement and sure enough there were keys, lots of keys, but none of them fit the lock on the box.

"Rats, I was hoping we could get into the box. Why would anyone lock the box unless there was something valuable in there? This is going to drive me nuts. Let's ask the boys at dinner tonight; maybe they can pick the lock. Okay, let's get back at it, girls."

I couldn't really focus on scavenging because I also wanted to know what was in the box. That's all I really thought about while I was going through boxes of junk, including more chipped dishes and old moth-eaten clothes.

Maggie was excited about some of the fabrics that she could use for quilting projects this winter. Carrie found some delightful old hats, some with feathers, some with velvet flowers, a few straw hats with velvet streamers that little girls wore to church on Sundays. She modeled each hat for us.

"Those hats would be really cute hung on a wall," Maggie said. "Great potential for the Artsy-Fartsy sale. We could each wear one for a start."

We surveyed our loot, but I could only focus on the mystery box.

Nick and Eric arrived about six to have a casual supper of brats on the grill and homemade kraut, along with potato salad, sliced tomatoes and cukes, and our home canned dills.

The "boys" had brought chocolate cake for dessert.

That kraut — my goodness what a process.

A few weeks ago after we had harvested ten heads of cabbage, we decided to make kraut, using another of Maggie's finds: an old-fashioned cabbage grater. One end of the grater sat on a chair and the other end sat with the grater blades over a large Red Wing crock. I straddled the chair end and put the washed cabbage in the wooden box attached to the grater and slid it across the blades. The grated cabbage fell into the clean crock. We added salt, covered the cabbage with a clean dish towel and weighted it down. We waited, checking it every day, until it started to ferment which meant I had to skim off the foam every day for weeks until it stopped bubbling.

I felt enslaved to the damn stinky stuff. I had no idea

it would be so much work for only three quarts of kraut. Amazing. I would never take kraut for granted again.

Before Nick and Eric could tackle the grilling, Maggie, Carrie, and I demanded they solve our problem: how to get into the mystery box without breaking it.

"Maggie, do you have a bobby pin?" Maggie took one from her hair and gave it to Nick.

He fiddled with the lock, but no luck.

"How about a paper clip?" She ran into the house and came back with the clip.

More fiddling.

"Voila! Success!" He held up the box.

"Were you a criminal in a former life?" I asked.

"Is there something I should know?" Maggie asked with a grin.

"Other than my time in the pen? Nah," Nick said.

Carrie reached for the box, but stopped and looked at me. "Suze, you found it. You get to open it first."

I was genuinely impressed with the kid, thinking of me like that.

"Thanks, kid. It will be my pleasure."

Suspense was in the air. Everyone stared at me, waiting for me to open the box. "Will it be jewelry worth a small fortune? Maybe money? Maybe stocks or bonds?"

"Or a kid's dead pet like a canary or kitten?" Carrie volunteered.

"Thanks a lot, Sis. Now I'm not so sure I want to open it."

I immediately thought of Pandora's box from Greek mythology. Curious, Pandora opened the box against Zeus's wishes and let out all of the bad and ugly things in the world like greed, cruelty, jealousy. The last thing in the box was hope, so in honor of hope, I opened the box ... to find three bundles of letters, each tied in a pink satin ribbon.

"Rats! We're not going to be rich," Maggie said.

"I'll bet they're love letters from a forbidden love. Maybe one of them is married. Maybe they're having an illicit affair and she has hidden the letters away from her husband's prying eyes," I said.

"Maybe she has a pen pal from a faraway country," Carrie said.

"Why don't we end the suspense and each take a few and read them," Maggie suggested.

"Nope, they're my letters — my treasure. I want to read them first. Then maybe we can share."

"I have no problems with that. If you like the box so much, why don't you keep it. It would be great to use as a Memory Box."

"I don't care about the letters. Anyway I can't even read cursive," Carrie said.

"Now that that's settled, let's get grilling," Nick said.

We had a fine supper as usual: good food, good conversation, I think, though I wasn't always tuned into it. Throughout the evening, I found myself thinking about those letters. Who were they from? Who were they to? And why did the person leave them locked in a box?

"Suze, Suze," Eric said, trying to get my attention. "We're heading out."

"Sorry, Eric, I'm a bit preoccupied with those letters."

"No kidding! You've been pretty much 'out of here' ever since you opened the box."

"I know I have, but I'm really stoked about reading those letters."

"I wouldn't want to keep you," Eric said as he walked away.

He's in a snit, Girl. Whatcha gonna do about it?

Nick was saying good-bye to Maggie and Carrie.

"Wait," I said, running to give him a hug and a kiss. He gave me a big Eric grin, so we were "good."

You're catchin' on, Girl.

"Keep me posted on the letters. I love a good mystery."

"Me too. Talk to you tomorrow with a full report."

CHAPTER 32

The Letters

July 1964

"Thanks for the dinner, Maggie. I'm heading upstairs to read the letters. I can hardly wait."

"Let me know what you find out."

"Will, do."

"Carrie, time for your bath," Maggie said. Carrie was coloring and didn't want to be disturbed.

"Do I have to? I helped wash the dishes. I'm already clean," Carrie said.

"Not good enough. No arguing allowed." Carrie followed Maggie and me up the steps, grumbling all the way.

"When you're done with 'em, will you tell us about the letters? Please?" Carrie asked.

"Sure thing, Sis."

Apparently there were many people curious about those letters, but no one more curious than me. Since I had showered that afternoon, I got into my pajamas and got ready to read. I had been thinking all evening about how to approach this. There were three bundles of letters: the first, from Gerald Carter to Louisa May

Johnson (the LMJ carved on the box?); second, from Louisa to Gerald and third, from Iris Hanson to Louisa.

I was hoping to put together a story line by alternating letters according to date, but that didn't work because Louisa wrote more often than Gerald, so I started with Louisa's bundle. Then I'd move to Gerald's letters and end with Iris's. That seemed the simplest.

My goals were to find out their stories and the circumstances around their communication (why the locked box?) and finally what happened to them all after the letters stopped. I hoped that's what the third bundle would tell me.

It was clear from Louisa's first letter to Gerald, dated November 20, 1942, that they were in a loving relationship and that Gerald had enlisted in the Army, much to Louisa's dismay. He had been sent to Cornwall in the UK.

She wrote about high school, her activities, her friends, and her chores on the Johnson farm. She hated being confined to the farm when there was "so much in the world to see." She missed him (a lot of mushy stuff here) and wished she could be with him.

The letters continued in that high school romantic way for many months until they stopped being romantic and started being angry. When I started reading Gerald's letters, I understood why.

His early letters emphasized how much he missed home and her. He complained about the UK weather, ("It rains a lot and is cold and damp most of the time."), the strange differences in language like biscuit (cookie), tea (supper), chips (French fries), jumper (sweater), jacket potato (baked potato). Also, "The Brits couldn't make a decent cup of coffee, but their beer was great."

In later letters, he started talking about the British girls who loved getting presents from American soldiers. "They'd give you a kiss for a candy bar."

In another letter he said that air-raid shelters were a great way "to pick up girls." He no longer used terms of endearment like "Sweetheart" or "Dearest." There were fewer "Xs" and "Os" until they stopped altogether.

The frequency of communication diminished to just a few letters a month and eventually stopped in the summer of 1943. This was the last letter Louisa received:

Dear Louisa,

I'm sorry, but I will no longer be writing to you. I've met someone else and will marry her when and if I return from Germany. I never meant to hurt you or for this to happen. You have been faithful and true. Please forgive me.

Gerald

No wonder Louisa was angry; she'd been dumped by her beloved soldier boy. They both sounded so young in their letters. She hated her life on the farm and romanticized a life married to Gerald. I wondered if Gerald made it through the war. I hoped Louisa found someone else to love. Maybe the third bundle of letters would answer those questions.

In Iris's first letter, dated June 10, 1944, she congratulated Louisa on her high school graduation. She also sent $5 dollars and her love. She signed it Aunt Iris.

Iris was apparently single and worked in a St. Paul law office as a secretary and lived in a small apartment on Lexington Avenue. She suggested that Louisa spend some time with her because Iris was certain she could find her a job working in the same office complex. They could share expenses if it was something she'd be interested in. Louisa jumped at the chance. The letters stopped in July of 1944.

I really wanted to find out what happened to these people. After reading all their letters, I felt like I knew them.

* * *

"Maggie, what do think I should do next? I want to find out what happened to these people. And why did Louisa put the letters in a locked box? And who sent Louisa's letters back to her?"

"Since you have her old address, why not write her a letter? You might get lucky and she'll still be there."

"Can't hurt. I'll do it."

So I went back to my room and introduced myself to Iris Hanson.

> Dear Miss Hanson,
>
> My name is Suzan Bailey and I live with my Aunt Maggie Thomas in the Johnson's old house on Nicolai Avenue outside of Miesville and south of Hastings.
>
> While searching the hay loft, I found a box with the initials LMJ on it. In the box were three bundles of letters: one from Gerald Carter, one from Louisa Johnson and one from you. The letters were of a personal nature.
>
> I'm wondering what happened to Gerald, Louisa and you, of course, and why the letters

*were in the box and who gave Louisa's letters
back to her.*

*Most importantly, I want to return the letters
to their rightful owners.*

Please contact me if you get this letter.

Sincerely,

Suzan Bailey

One week later I got a reply. That became the beginning of my pen pal relationship with Iris.

Chapter 33

More Letters

August 1964

> *Dear Miss Bailey,*
>
> *I was shocked and thrilled to receive your letter. Shocked that those letters still existed and thrilled that Louisa might get them back. In my opinion, Louisa never really got over Gerald.*
>
> *Unfortunately, Gerald was seriously wounded while overseas and returned home permanently damaged. He died several years later. She saw him twice before he took his life. War leaves many casualties.*
>
> *She and I lived together for about four years until she fell for one of our young lawyers, got married, and moved to Illinois. We exchange Christmas cards, but that's about it. She's a busy mother and housewife now.*
>
> *I would love to meet with you in person at your convenience and tell you all that I know about Louisa and her family.*

Sincerely,

Iris Hanson

P.S. Why were you "searching" the hay loft? Just curious.

Dear Miss Hanson,

Thanks for your letter explaining what happened to Gerald. How very sad. Did you know him well? Did his family return Louisa's letters to her?

I was surprised that you actually got my letter. Twenty years is a long time to be living in the same place. I hit the jackpot actually connecting with you!

I now realize that "searching" was a weird way to explain how I found the box, but my aunt, sister, and I have found a lot of "treasures" in the barn loft that we have re-purposed and intend to sell at our Arts and Crafts sale later this month. When we finally set the date, I'll let you know. Then maybe we can have a face-to-face chat. I'd like that. My mom and dad will be helping with the sale and you could meet them and the rest of the family.

I'm looking forward to a possible meeting someday. Too bad I can't drive. My parents won't let me until I turn eighteen! Only another year to wait and then watch out world!

Sincerely,

Suze,

(It's okay for you to call me by my first name.)

Dear Suze,

Good to hear from you. I like writing letters, especially to a young woman interested in my family history.

You expressed some surprise about my living arrangements. When I first moved to St. Paul, I found a job in the law office (where I am now, recently promoted to Office Manager) and a small apartment where I lived for almost ten years, but I felt I needed a bit more space, so when a larger two-bedroom apartment became available in the same building, I took it.

Fortunately, the mailman recognized the name and put it in my box. So I hit the jackpot as well!

Now, as for Gerald ... I only knew him through Louisa and her family. Her parents thought she was way too young to get serious, especially with someone who intended to enlist. They didn't approve, so I imagine she tried to hide the letters from their prying eyes.

Stephen, her older brother and my nephew, made the box and presented it to her on her 17th birthday. Both Stephen and Gerald, buddies since childhood, enlisted shortly thereafter. I suspect he and Gerald were in cahoots about keeping Gerald's letters secret. A locked box was perfect. I can venture a guess that it was Gerald's parents who returned Louisa's letters and she added them to her memory box.

Later she chose to leave the letters and the box behind. She was still angry and hurt about the break-up and probably wanted to move on and put all of it behind her. That's my theory anyway.

In case you're interested, Stephen Johnson still lives in the vicinity, I believe in Red Wing. He also came back damaged from the war (who didn't?) and became rather reclusive. To my knowledge he never married or had children.

I haven't seen him for years.

Well, I plan on coming to see your re-purposed treasures the weekend of August 22-23. It will probably be on Sat. the 22nd. I'll be the one wearing the red carnation. Ha!

Until then, let's continue to write. Tell me a bit about yourself and your family. This is fun!

Sincerely,

Iris

Dear Iris,

You're right. This is fun!

You asked if I'd be interested in finding Stephen. I would and I would like to invite him to our sale on the 22nd. Would you mind?

You asked about my family. I imagine you're curious about why my sister and I are living with Aunt Maggie. Mom and Dad were having "marital difficulties" and needed to get away from Carrie and me. And we sure needed to get away from them! We called their "marital difficulties" the Mom and Dad Wars. They're going to counseling right now and seem to be getting along much better.

Aunt Maggie is wonderful; she lives in what Carrie named the Rainbow House. You'll see why we call it that when you visit. She has animals, including pigs named Peggy Sue and Pickles, chickens, a goat, and dogs and cats.

She has a massive garden and sells her produce every weekend, so plan on taking home some veggies and homemade pickles when you visit. Both Carrie and I help around the farm and garden as much as we can.

This summer has been unreal. I've learned lots about plants and animals and how to take care of them. Maggie's taught me to can, cook, and bake.

I've learned a lot about my family and myself. It will be hard to leave and go back to boring old St. Cloud, but I will be happy to see my friends again and go back to school. This year I'll be taking American History. I want to learn all I can about WWII. Just reading Louisa and Gerald's letters, talking to Mom ,who lost her first love in the war, and writing to you has made a big difference, so thank you.

See you soon! We've got tons of neat stuff to sell, but don't feel any pressure to buy.

Your friend,

Suze

Dear Suze,

My goodness, dear, you're busy. You have certainly learned a lot this summer about nature and about life. I could feel your enthusiasm for Aunt Maggie, her menagerie, her garden, her Rainbow House. I can hardly wait to meet her and her critters. You've really piqued my curiosity.

I could never understand why people thought history was boring. Maybe it's because teachers taught only the facts and ignored the real people living and loving within the facts. Your personal connection with the war and its casualties, civilian and military alike, will definitely help in your class. Challenge your teacher to include the every day people who are living the history. I see a budding history teacher in the making, the kind of teacher who will ignite and nurture curiosity through personal connections.

I'd like to make a suggestion of a book to read that was one of my favorites: The Winds of War by Herman Wouk. It's long but worth it. Drama, romance, sex, family tension all set in a backdrop of the war.

Good luck in your preparations for the Arts and Crafts sale coming up soon. I look forward to meeting your family and seeing the treasures you've discovered in the barn. Another bonus might be Stephen. I would love to connect with my nephew. Thanks for thinking of us.

Be safe and happy, dear friend.

Iris

Dear Iris,

Please save all my letters and return them to me whenever you wish. I want to fill Louisa's memory box with all the wonderful things that have happened this summer.

Here's what I've put in so far: Carrie's "Poppy the Penguin" story that I forgot to return to her, my dried birthday corsage from Eric, my birthday cards, the boxes that held the ring from Maggie and the locket from Eric, my bowling score from our first date, many Polaroid pictures, and your letters.

I know you'll want to know all about Eric and you'll meet him when you visit. He's the best.

Love,

Suze

CHAPTER 34

Artsy-Fartsy Prep

August, 1964

"Okay, kids, we've got only a few weeks to pull everything together for our Artsy-Fartsy sale."

"Sorry to interrupt, Maggie, but I think you need a classier name for advertising purposes. We can still call it the Artsy-Fartsy sale among ourselves, but we don't want our customers to get the wrong idea. How about Maggie's Arts and Crafts Sale? It goes with Maggie's Veggie Stand."

"But it's not just my stuff. This has been a team effort."

"Then how 'bout Rainbow House Arts and Crafts Sale?" Carrie suggested.

"Not bad. The house could be our logo. Good job, sweetie. Is that okay with the rest of you?"

"Ya, you betcha!" Eric said.

I agreed, but I liked the original name 'cause it was weird and fun, kind of like the stuff we were trying to sell.

"First, we need to inventory exactly what we have and then make a list of projects to be completed. We also need to find a place to have the sale that will give us the most exposure."

"Why not our yard? People are used to seeing our veggies and flowers, so when they come to buy veggies, they'll see our art and re-purposed furniture. It will be easy to arrange everything 'cause we don't have to transport our stuff somewhere else," I said.

"How about the empty gas station close to King's? Maybe we could get permission to set up there," Maggie said. "There's a lot of traffic going right past that station. We might get some drive-by interest. If I bribe you with more good suppers, would you and your dad help move stuff in the truck?"

"Sure. We'd be glad to help. But honestly I agree with Suze," Eric said. "We don't want to ignore our regular customers. Maybe next year when the sale has established itself we can look for another place."

"You're probably right. We've got a lot going on," Maggie said. "And it would be much easier to display the stuff here. Less hassle all around. Maybe we just need to advertise better. An ad in the Hastings and Cannon Falls paper? More signs for sure. Emma and Jake will be here to help that weekend. As much as I hate to mention it, that's also the weekend you girls will be going home to St. Cloud," Maggie said, wrinkling her nose in disgust. Eric and I made grumpy faces. Not Carrie, Little Miss Happy Face.

"Mom said I could take Berry with me," Carrie said with a grin. At least someone seemed happy about moving back.

It seemed like we just got here. I decided not to think about it and just concentrate on enjoying the time I had left at the Rainbow House.

"So what have we got to sell that doesn't need work?"

"The little blue dresser? Should we cutesy it up for a baby or child's room or just clean it up?"

"Let's table that decision. If we have some extra time, we might look at the cutesy option. Otherwise, I say let's clean and oil it and see how it looks."

"The doll cradle you found, Maggie, might be good for the child's room theme. Do you have a doll we could add?"

"Sure, I do. I found an old rag doll at a garage sale, now sitting on a shelf in my room. That would work. We could sell the doll and cradle together. I've also made about a dozen throw pillows of various sizes from those housedresses and the table cloths we found. Good thing those ladies were sturdy," Maggie said with a grin.

"There are quite a few broken chairs out in the barn. We can check them out," Eric said.

"You've never been scavenging before with us. It's a blast! When we're done in the barn, we can take Eric to the dump. Last time we went we didn't have a big, strong, manly-man to help us lift heavy things," I said, and Eric flexed his muscles to prove his manly-manness.

We found six chairs in various stages of disrepair and put them in the yard so we could imagine what to do with them.

"Do they still have to be chairs?" Carrie asked. "Or can we take them apart?"

"Great idea, Carrie." Maggie walked around looking at the chairs with fresh eyes. "What if we separated the top from the seat or better yet, we could use part of the seat to make a neat shelf. We could paint it to match the small dresser. Or *not*. Look at this chair. It has a nicely shaped back and would make an interesting shelf. I'd buy that," Maggie said.

"Once we've separated the top from the chair seat, Maggie could upholster a new seat to make a bench or we could skip the upholstering and paint the whole thing and make an end table."

"Now what could we do with the legs? This chair, for example has great legs, but the rest of the chair is crappy."

"How about we remove each of the legs and paint them different colors, like the Rainbow House, and make them into candle holders. Look at the cool legs on this one."

"I've lots of dibs and dabs of paint we could use," Maggie said. "You kids are coming up with great ideas."

We went to each chair and discussed possibilities. Eric set aside two of the really bad chairs to take home to experiment with.

"Sounds to me like a trip to the dump for more chairs. Girls, go change to long pants and long sleeved shirts 'cause we're heading into SquitoLand." Eric was already wearing jeans and a rolled up long-sleeved shirt so he was prepared. He also brought a screw driver and a pliers from the barn "just in case."

"To the dump! To the dump!" Carrie started to chant as she marched from the kitchen to the yard in her scavenging clothes.

"Look for old weathered wood and door knobs or drawer pulls. I've got the manly-man tools to remove them from the drawers. I'm getting tons of ideas for hook rack things, wooden Christmas trees from spindles, picture frames. Let's go. I'm pumped for the dump!" Eric said.

"To the dump!" Carrie took up the battle cry and we were off.

We weren't disappointed. Once we braved the ravine and the "squirrels," we found a neat old wooden door (a table perhaps?), a typewriter table, four wooden soda crates, plus some weathered barn wood and a few abandoned dresser drawers that had neat hardware on them.

Just as we were getting ready to leave, Carrie found three rusted Christmas tree stands of different sizes that she insisted we take back with us. What could we ever do with those? I was still trying to wrap my brain around the spindle Christmas trees Eric has suggested.

"Let's each take what we can carry and Suze and I will bring the wheelbarrows for the rest, though that heavy wooden door is going to be tricky."

"Maybe your dad can help tonight. He's coming for supper. I made goulash."

"Num," Carrie said. "I love noodles and hamburger."

"Eric, how are you with making picture frames?"

"Never made any, but I can learn with Dad's help." He stopped and looked back over his shoulder. "Come to think about it, I thought I saw a few frames back in the ravine. Wait a sec; I'll be right back." Eric ran back to the dump and returned with two frames and an old mirror. He also returned with a nasty scratch on his hand.

"What happened?" Maggie said when she saw he was bleeding.

"That must hurt," I said.

"Not much. I must have scratched myself on that

rusty saw, reaching for the mirror. I'll wash it off when I get back to the house."

"Are you up to date on your tetanus shot?"

"Don't know. Maybe Dad would. I know we had to get a complete physical before we could play baseball. I did got some shots then, but I don't remember what they were."

"We'll give it a good wash and a dose of merthiolate, when we get home."

"Ouch. That stuff stings."

"Don't worry, Eric, I'll hold your hand. Be brave, my manly-man," I told him.

"He's my manly-man, too," Carrie said.

CHAPTER 35

Field Trip

August 1964

After rereading my correspondence from Iris, I had an idea. I wanted to find her nephew, Stephen Johnson, who supposedly lived in Red Wing, and invite him to our sale on the 22nd. Maybe he and Iris could connect, become friends, have a miniature family reunion. But before I wrote to him, I needed to research if he was still alive and if so, where he lived. What better place to do that than the library. My second reason for wanting a library field-trip was to check out *The Winds of War,* by Herman Wouk, Iris's recommendation.

I knew the Squirt also wanted to go and see what the Hindenberg looked like. Ever since Mom carved on that zeppelin-like zucchini, Carrie has been asking to see pictures of the "big balloon that carried people." Next time Maggie had to go to town for supplies, we would go with her and check out the library.

Imagine our shock to go into Hastings and find that the library was in the basement of 507 Vermillion St., an ugly businesslike building, and it was closed. The sign said : "Open Mondays, Wednesdays, and Fridays from eleven to four." It was Tuesday. Bummer.

Compared to the St. Cloud Library, a majestic yellow brick and granite building with fireplaces inside and a special room for kids' books, Hastings didn't even have a real library.

"Maggie, is this really the library?" Carrie asked. "It doesn't look like a library."

"Yes, kids, it is, but we're getting a new library at another location in just a few months. We'll all have to come back when it's finished. I know you wanted to check out a book, but there is a used book store in town where we can probably find *The Winds of War,* so no worries there, Suze."

"Good." I really wanted to start that book, so that Iris and I could discuss it. Good thing I'd have my own copy, because it was long and I doubted that I could have finished before I had to go home.

I felt sorry for Hastings' kids not having a nice library. When I was a kid about Carrie's age, Mom and I would take the bus downtown and walk to the library located on Fifth Avenue after having lunch at either Dan Marsh Drug Store or Inga's Café.

I would get as many books as they'd allow me to get so that I could become a member of the Mad Hatter's Club. I continued to visit the library on a regular basis all the way through elementary and junior high. Now our high school has a pretty good library of its own, so I don't get to the public library as much.

When we got back to Rainbow House, Eric was busy working in the garden. He had parked his truck close to the barn so he could easily unload some of his repurposed chair creations. He welcomed us with a big ol' Eric grin, dimples and all.

"How was the library? Did you get what you needed?"

"Nope, it wasn't open. Wrong day, wrong time. But the good news is I found the book I wanted at the used book store, so it didn't cost much."

"Looks like you've been busy, Eric," Maggie said when she spotted Eric's boxes in the back of his truck. "Show me what you've got."

Eric brought out one shelf, one hook thingy, and eight candle-holders of various heights.

"I thought I'd leave the painting decisions to you guys. I had to add some pieces of wood to top off the candle holders, to make them safer for candles. Actually, I think they're cool to set on a shelf or mantle. I had to do some sanding, but not a lot. And I added wood to the chair back to make the hook thingy. What do you call those hook thingys anyway?"

"Haven't a clue. I like 'hook thingys' myself."

"They're handy to have for clothes, towels, keys. I think they'll sell."

"Eric, you're a genius." Maggie gave Eric a hug. "How's the hand, by the way?"

"I asked Dad about the tetanus shot and he said I was up to date. No worries there. I washed it again and changed the bandage. I'll live. So what's next, ladies?"

"How do you feel about taking home a few more chairs? Maybe two more 'hook thingys' and a couple of benches or tables. I might upholster or paint them, not sure. Well, kids, we're on our way to repurposing junk. I love it."

"Oh, Suze, did you find out anything about Stephen Johnson?" Eric grinned like he was hiding something.

"Nope. Any ideas?"

"Well, I found this old Red Wing telephone book of Dad's. Ta-Da!" Eric handed me the old telephone book he was hiding behind his back. "There were a few Johnsons you could check out."

"What will I ever do without you?"

Suddenly I realized that my days at the Rainbow House were numbered. I wouldn't be seeing Eric every day. Or Maggie, or the animals. I started to cry.

"Come here, you," Eric said as he enveloped me in his manly-man arms.

"Can't stand around snuggling and cuddling all day when there's work to be done," Maggie said.

"Carrie and I will be out in the barn, painting your beautiful creations. Come on, Suze, we need your expert advice."

"I'll be there in a sec. I need to check the Red Wing phone book for Stephen Johnson."

"Good luck. I hope you find him. Eric, could you come take a look at the weathered barn wood we scavenged? I was thinking of using those glass knobs from the dresser drawers instead of hooks for those 'hook thingys.' What do you think of making the drawers into book shelves?"

When I looked in the phone book, I found ten Johnsons listed, but only one Steve Johnson. I called the number, but no one was home. I decided to write after supper, rather than phone again, since I could do a more thorough job explaining the situation and my motives for contacting him. And it was cheaper to use the post office instead of long distance.

If he is the right Stephen Johnson. If he writes back and agrees to meet Iris, I'll give her a quick call. I would really like to reunite those two.

In the meantime, I'll try to squeeze in as much "snuggling" and "cuddling" as possible.

I suspect Miss Maggie has been doing the same with Mr. Nick. I caught them mid-cuddle just last week when the boys were over for dinner.

Sneaky, sneaky.

CHAPTER 36

Blue Ribbons

August 1964

Maggie delivered her pickles to the Dakota County Fairgrounds in Farmington, Minnesota a week before the fair opened. She had entered every year for the past three years and had yet to win anything.

We went to the fair early in the morning of August 14th to check out the pickle judging and the rest of the fair, too, of course. I was genuinely puzzled about why anyone would want to go to the trouble of entering pickles (or anything else for that matter) in a county fair. Maybe I would find out.

"I bet you won!" Carrie said as we were getting into the car. "Can I go on the merry-go-round after we see if you won? I want hot dogs and cotton candy too." The eighteen miles to Farmington should go fast with her blabberings.

"What do you want to see, Suze?" Maggie said.

"I love the animals and the arts and crafts more than the rides and games."

"Me too," Maggie said.

"Are we there yet? I have to go to the bathroom,"

Carrie said. Typical Carrie. I told her to go right before we left, but she gave me her usual, "I don't have to. You're not the boss of me."

"It's just the excitement, honey. You'll be fine. We'll be there in about fifteen minutes."

The weather was perfect for the fair: sunny, a slight breeze, not too hot or humid. A few blocks before parking we could hear the calliope music and smell fried food mixed with a variety of animal smells, mostly cow and horse manure. Since we were here so early, we actually found a decent parking spot. We wanted to see the exhibits before the crowds got too big and the lines too long.

Living in the country for just a few months, I had refined my olfactory palette. I could actually differentiate between kinds of poop. I'd become a feces connoisseur. Horse and cow poop wasn't bad; in fact, I found it rather pleasant, wholesome even. Now pig poop, on the other hand, was sharp, sour, plug-your-nose harsh. After smelling the neighbor's pig farm, up close and personal, I declared pig poop the worst. If I were a judge at the fair, I would give pig poop the blue ribbon for Rude Stinkiness. That expertise alone should add to my popularity once I go back to St. Cloud.

Walking to the animal barn, I realized just how fond of Maggie's menagerie I'd become. Every day those critters made me laugh. Just yesterday I saw Mrs. Minniver jump on Peggy Sue's back and ride around the yard, clucking all the way. Last night after supper Buddy Holly butted Eric in the butt when he was bent over weeding. The cats were always doing something naughty like hiding in the barn and jumping out and attacking the dogs.

Berry would hide in the laundry basket and attack whenever anyone walked by. I'm not sure taking her home with us is the best idea. She'll miss her freedom and her animal pals, plus she'll drive Mom crazy with her antics, to say nothing of her mousie and hairball gifts.

"Look at that big ol' pig, Suze," Carrie said. "His name is Rupert. See? I can read the sign."

"Good job, sweetie. Wow, those are huge *chibongas*," Maggie said, laughing.

"There's that funny word you guys were talking about," Carrie said, reaching down to scratch Rupert.

"When was that, Sis?"

"You know, right before Rudy's funeral."

"I remember now."

"What are *chibongas*, Maggie?"

"That one's yours to answer," I said, walking away to where the sheep were penned. A few minutes later Carrie and Maggie joined me. Carrie pointed to a ram and said, "Look at his huge *chibongas*, Suze."

Way to go, Maggie.

After the Sex Ed lesson, we headed to the Midway for the rides and the food. Even though we had a small breakfast before we left, all those good smells got to us and we succumbed to hot dogs with the works, mini donuts, and cotton candy.

"Can we go on the Ferris wheel, Maggie, please? Pretty please with mustard on it?"

"Speaking of mustard, you have some on your face." Maggie handed Carrie a napkin.

"How about we start with the Merry Go Round and see how that goes?"

"That's for little kids who get scared. I'm not scared

and I wanna go high in the sky and look around like a bird. Please, Maggie. I promise I won't get scared."

"What do your think, Suze? Can she do it?"

"She can, but I'm not so sure that I can. I hate heights."

"Suze-is-a scaredy-cat," Carrie started to sing.

"I can't believe I'm being pressured by an 8-year-old, but what the hay, I'll try it."

"Yay! We're going on the Ferris wheel."

We bought our tickets and waited in line. Because Carrie was eight, she had to sit with Maggie and I took the seat across from them. We got into the gondola (I asked the carnie worker what it was called) and buckled in. Immediately, Carrie started rocking it.

"Carrie, the man just told us we shouldn't rock the gondola. Knock it off."

She gave me "The Look."

The gondola started to move slowly at first and then as we got higher and higher it started to move faster. The view from the top was amazing — beautiful, scary, and exciting.

Carrie squealed in delight as she pointed out everything. "Look at, look at, look at..." Then I looked at Maggie who, with each rotation, was turning another shade of gray/green.

When we finally got off, Maggie ran to the nearest trash barrel and lost her lunch. I bought her a 7-Up, got her to sit down, and finally her color returned to normal.

"Let's just rest here a few minutes. What happened?"

"I thought I'd outgrown getting sick on the Ferris wheel. Guess not."

"I'm happy you didn't barf on me."

"There's always something to be grateful for, Carrie," Maggie said.

"It's okay, Maggie. I barf sometimes too," Carrie said, taking Maggie's hand. "Are you feeling better?"

"Yes, hon, much. Let's go see how my pickles did and then we can head on home."

"I know you're going to win, Maggie. That will make you feel much, much better."

When we got to the 4-H building where all the food and produce judging took place, we found Maggie's pickles quite easily because her jar of dills got a blue ribbon and so did her bread and butters.

"Maggie, you're the pickle queen! Congrats!" We each gave her a big hug.

"I can't believe I won. The same lady, Eileen Swanson, wins every year. I don't see her mentioned at all."

"That's because she died," a voice from behind us said. We turned and saw an old, stoop-shouldered man with tears in his eyes. "She was my wife and the best pickle maker in Dakota County."

The ride home was quiet mainly because Carrie had fallen asleep in the back seat and Maggie and I were saddened by the news of Eileen Swanson's death. Talk about letting the air out of our balloons.

I was beginning to understand why people entered fair competitions. For a brief moment fair-goers and judges honored the hard work and creativity of rural men and women. They'd get recognized and appreciated for what they do every day. I knew how hard Maggie worked to keep her hobby farm going, to keep her treasured lifestyle going. If a few Blue Ribbons helped her feel appreciated and valued it was well worth it. And I was grateful to be a part of it.

We were tired, dusty, ready for baths and a healthy meal, made from Maggie's veggies not something thrown into a deep fryer. I decided to make us dinner after we rested and cleaned up.

"Dinner's on me tonight, Maggie. I'm making us BLTs, green beans from the garden, and ice cream with your raspberry jam as a topping."

"Sounds great! I'm tired out from all that fair excitement. I think I'll go upstairs and relax, maybe read some of your book if you don't mind."

"Go ahead. I'll call you when supper's ready."

"Carrie, I need you to pick us green beans for supper." No answer. I looked in the front yard, no Carrie. The backyard, no Carrie. The garden, no Carrie. So I checked the hay loft and there she was, going through several boxes of stuff we hadn't yet explored.

"Whatcha doin', Squirt?"

"I'm checking out more boxes for the Artsy-Fartsy Sale. Come see what I've found."

"More treasures, I see." I looked at the contents: some coins in a silver box, a stamp book, a complete set of Raggedy Ann and Andy books, and some pots and pans. Some looked to be copper. "Sis, I think you've hit it big! Let's take these inside and show Maggie when she comes down for supper. She's resting upstairs at the moment. I told her we'd make supper. Come on, Sis, I'll help you carry stuff."

"Maggie's *resting?*"

"Weird, huh."

After supper Eric and Nick dropped by to show us what they'd created using the door and the four Coke crates from the dump. Carrie and I shared our new treasures with them. Nick thought the coins and stamps might be worth something and asked to take them to a friend who collected both.

Carrie begged to keep the Raggedy Ann and Andy books and Maggie wanted to clean the copper pans and hang them in her kitchen.

Now for the boys' treasures: Three of the four Coke crates and salvaged barn wood magically became an end table, and the old door was transformed into a smashing dining table. These guys were repurposing geniuses.

"We just scraped the paint from the table, sanded it a bit, and then varnished it. Dad made the rest from salvaged wood. I think it's pretty cute," Eric said, proud of their work.

"Cute? You guys are cute. The table is fabulous," I said.

"I love the end table with the red Coke crates," Maggie said when she pulled out the top crate from the table. "What a great place for storing stuff. Weren't there four Coke crates?"

"You betcha there were." Nick went to the truck and took out the last crate. "Ta da! A spice rack for Maggie's kitchen! And we didn't have to do a thing. You can either lean it against the wall or actually nail it to the wall."

"The red lettering is perfect." We all traipsed into the kitchen and nailed it into place. Maggie immediately went to her spice drawer and started filling the crate with spices.

"And we have another surprise," Nick said. "I'll be right back."

Nick ran back to the truck and came in with a bottle of sparkling wine and a bottle of sparkling apple juice for "the kids."

"A little bird told me about some Blue Ribbons. Get out the juice glasses, I mean the wine glasses."

"A toast to the best pickle maker in Dakota County. To Maggie!"

Maggie and I both got teary eyed.

"A toast to Eileen Swanson," Maggie said.

"She died," Carrie said and we all laughed.

"To Eileen."

CHAPTER 37

Sale Countdown

August 1964

"Nick, can you think of a way we can display those hook and shelf thingys? They would look so much better hanging up." Maggie was on the phone with Nick. "Just a sec." She went into the hall closet, dragging the phone cord with her. If I hadn't witnessed it with my own eyes, I wouldn't have believed an adult behaving so much like a lovesick teenager. I only moved into the closet twice talking to Eric.

"Whatcha doin' in the closet, Maggie?" Carrie asked. Maggie giggled.

"Shush, she's sweet-talking with Nick and wants some privacy."

"*Ohh.*" Carrie rolled her eyes. "Maggie and Nicky sitting in a tree-ee, K-I-S-S—I-N-G."

A few minutes later Maggie emerged from the closet with a gleam in her eye. She mumbled into the phone, "Me too."

As a lovesick teenager myself, I knew the code: "Me too" was an answer to "I love you," "I miss you," "I need you," "I want you," etc. when there were big or little ears around. Unfortunately for Maggie, she had both.

"Nick is going to experiment with ways to hang stuff

up. Like the hook things and my watercolors. He and Eric have been such a help with this sale. I don't know what we'd do without them."

At the thought of going home to St. Cloud and all that I would miss here, most of all Eric, I started to cry. Maggie just held me. "I'm going to miss you and Carrie so much. You have been an amazing help and support. I love you guys."

"Me, too," I said and we both laughed.

* * *

Five Days to Sale

Eric and Nick continue to do the carpentry work that we don't have the tools or the skills to accomplish.

Suze feeds and waters the animals, not her favorite chore.

Carrie and Maggie make watercolor stationery and paintings. Carrie specializes in pigs and cats, Maggie in bluebirds.

Suze paints the candle holders, hook and shelf thingys, and herself.

Maggie cooks, washes clothes, and gets the house ready for Mom and Dad.

Suze bakes five loaves of nummy zucchini bread and settles the animals for the night.

Maggie washes up after supper, snuggles with Nick on the front porch. Suze takes a walk with Eric before they leave.

We fall all into bed exhausted.

* * *

Four Days to Sale

Eric mows the lawn, weeds the garden, feeds and waters the animals. Yay!

Suze digs and washes potatoes and carrots, pulls beets and onions.

Carrie collects and washes vases for flowers and chases the animals namely the pigs and Mrs. Minniver.

Maggie sews one sleeveless shift dress in each of three sizes — small, medium, and large — to use as prototypes if anyone wants to order.

Nick delivers more stuff to paint and stays for supper. Suze and Carrie clean kitchen and bring up pickles, jams, and jellies from basement pantry.

Maggie crashes after supper. Suze and Eric snuggle on front porch.

* * *

Three Days to Sale

Eric and Nick frame, make signs. Eric feeds, waters animals.

Suze picks, washes veggies.

Maggie washes, changes bedding. Maggie gathers all that's for sale, puts on front porch.

It rains. Carrie plays, gets dirty. Leftovers for supper.

Maggie in bed with sore throat.

Eric and Suze cuddle.

* * *

Two Days to Sale

Mom and Dad arrive. Dad takes over animals. Mom takes over kitchen.

Carrie and Suze do garden stuff and paint.

Eric and Nick finish carpentry work.

Maggie in bed with bad cold. No cuddling allowed.

* * *

Suze Gets Letter

Dear Miss Bailey,

Thanks so much for your letter introducing yourself and explaining why you wanted to contact me. I've thought about it quite a bit and have decided to decline your offer. I don't go out much any more because of my war injuries.

Good luck with your arts and crafts sale and please feel free to give Aunt Iris my phone number and address. I would like to get in touch with her. She and my sister are my only family members left.

Sincerely,

Stephen Johnson

* * *

One Day to Sale

Dad and Mom do chores.
Carrie blabs.
Mom makes chicken soup.
Suze doesn't care about Nick and Eric.
Maggie and Suze sick.

* * *

"I'm not surprised you and Maggie are sick, the way you've been working. If you're going to be any use at all tomorrow, you'll have to stay in bed, sleep as much as you can and eat this," Mom said as she put the tray with soup, tea, and orange juice on the bedside table.

I ate and I drank.

"When I finish delivering the same to Maggie, including the advice, I'll come back for more instructions about what needs to be done."

"Thanks, Mom," I said, sneezing.

"God bless you" were the last words I heard before falling into a deep sleep.

* * *

"Oh, Eric, you look so handsome in Maggie's lavender print shift. It's just your color," I said to Eric as I was hanging up braids of carrots and onions on a pink and purple polka-dot hook thingy.

"Everything looks beautiful. I especially like the pig in the doll's bed. She looks so comfortable. Pickles, come to Mommy." Then Mom came from the house, holding her stomach like she was in pain.

"Sorry, Mommy, I can't help you because there's a lady wearing a red carnation that I should know, but I can't remember her name, and she's with a man who has a burned face and a missing leg. I know him too, but I don't remember his name either. It's on the box, the box, where I keep all my treasures. I have to find the box."

* * *

"Shush, darling, you were having a bad dream, something about finding 'the box,'" Mom said as she wiped my forehead with a cold washcloth.

And then I went back to sleep.

* * *

CHAPTER 38

Lift Off

August 1964

"How long was I asleep anyway?" I asked when I walked into the kitchen. Mom was making scrambled eggs and toast. Dad was in the barn.

"You slept most of the afternoon and all night. How are you feeling?"

"A bit like I've been run over, but I'll be okay when I have a cup of tea and some toast."

"When you've done that, take some aspirin. That should help with the aches."

"How is Maggie doing?"

"Better. She's out in the yard arranging things with Eric and Nick. Once the sale actually starts, we should be able to handle the customers, so you two can take it easy. Those men of yours have been a great help. I'm so happy we could all be here for you."

"Me, too." I started to give Mom a hug, but she put up her hands.

"I'd love a hug, but I don't want to get sick."

"Sorry, wasn't thinking." That meant no hugs or kisses for Eric either. *Way to muck up a good-bye, girl.*

At least I could hug Maggie since she was already contaminated.

I helped myself to aspirin, tea, toast, and a small helping of scrambled eggs. Now that I'd eaten, I started to feel slightly better. After my shower, I felt almost a hundred percent. Make that fifty percent.

"There she is!" Eric said, running up to me. "I've been worried about you."

"Stop! before I infect you."

"I think that's probably already happened. Besides I don't care." I gave Eric a big ol' hug and that felt better than the shower, the breakfast, *and* the aspirin.

"Dad has some news about the stuff Carrie found in the hay loft. I think you'll be surprised." Eric took my hand and we went to talk to Maggie and Nick.

"Dad, tell Suze about the appraisal."

"Well, I sure was shocked. The stamps and coins are worth something, quite a lot actually. Even the box is valuable because it's silver. Who knew? I probably would have taken the coins out and thrown the box away." He handed me the paper work. "I didn't want to sell them in case you wanted to do something else." By this time Carrie ran to join us.

"Whatcha talkin' about?"

"We found out what those 'treasures' you found in the hay loft are worth," Maggie said. "Nick was nice enough to get an appraisal from the experts."

"What's an appraisal?"

"It's a piece of paper that tells what something is worth."

"Does that mean I'm gonna be rich?" Carrie asked, jumping up and down. "Finders-keepers!"

"Hold your horses, kid. We'll talk about it at supper

tonight," Maggie said. "Meanwhile we have to finish getting ready for our customers. Sure hope the signs have worked their magic. Everything looks great, Team! Thank you so much. We'll settle up tonight with the finances. I want to give you your share."

I surveyed all of our work displayed with Maggie's eye for color and design. Eric and Nick did the heavy lifting, the carpentry work, and the transporting of the bigger pieces. Carrie and I helped scavenge, paint, and come up with ideas for the repurposing. It truly was a team effort and I was proud to be on the team.

They had arranged everything like outside rooms. Nick had designed walls made out of pegboard, so we could hang the watercolors and the hook thingys to show how the pieces could be used. One of the hook thingys was made with the top of a chair but instead of hooks Nick had used the glass knobs from the dresser drawers. Adding an old wooden hanger, Maggie hung one of her shifts on a glass knob alongside a cute watercolor sign that stated the sizes, prices and colors available. She was also modeling one, and wore one of the hats Carrie had found.

The shelving units made from dresser drawers had books, dishes, and flower bouquets displayed, all for sale. The dining room table was covered with candle holders and a pile of freshly washed and ironed table cloths. We had baskets of produce on the end tables and throw pillows made from the '30s housedresses on the painted chairs.

The baby room was especially charming. Maggie decided to paint one of her old wicker rockers a crisp white. She'd put two of her yellow and blue print pillows on the rocker. A shelf, again made from an old chair, had the Raggedy Ann and Andy books displayed. The pegboards were filled with Carrie and Maggie's watercolors. All that was needed to finish the room was a crib and a kid.

Around nine, exactly the time advertised, cars started to appear on the road. Eric directed them to parking areas on the lawn and across the road. Most of our customers started looking at our arts and crafts in the yard and then made their way to the roadside veggie stand. We were very busy at first, then it thinned out a bit right around lunch time, so we could have something to eat, use the bathrooms, etc.

Of course, the animals had to make an appearance — especially Buddy Holly, who in spite of our careful confinement strategies had escaped.

Instead of reacting negatively, the kids who came with their parents were charmed by the old goat. Carrie took them to the barn to show the kids Mrs. Minniver and her clucky pals, and the two pigs. The cats and dogs roamed freely, including the two fattest felines who decided to sprawl on the dining table, knocking over the few candle sticks we had left.

We advertised that the cats came with the table which might have explained the fact that it wasn't selling. To anyone interested, Nick offered to deliver the table, minus the cats, free of charge. *What a guy!*

Early in the afternoon I noticed an attractive older lady milling about our displays. When she turned around I saw the red carnation pinned to her blouse.

"Iris, you came!" I ran over to her. "I'd give you a hug, but I'm getting over a cold and don't want you to get it. Mom has warned me not to infect the customers."

"How about I blow you a kiss? Would that be okay with your mom?"

"I'm so glad you came. It must be kinda weird to see the property again. How long has it been?"

"I'm guessing about fifteen years or so. The place certainly has changed ... and for the better."

By this time, Eric had joined us. I introduced them.

"Nice to meet you," Eric said, shaking Iris's hand. Iris gave Eric the once over and then winked at me as if to say, "He's a keeper."

"Come here, you, and let me take a look. Other than the red nose, you're adorable." Then she looked around at the sale, the yard, the front garden and finally the house. "I can see why you like it here. Show me around."

"Well, this is the Rainbow House. You can see why Carrie named it that." Iris looked a little flabbergasted at all the colors, but she laughed.

"'There's no place like home.' This is an explosion of pure joy! Brilliant. It would be impossible to be depressed coming home to this every day! How lucky you are to be able to enjoy it. Now I want to see where all the beautiful vegetables and flowers come from."

Eric and I showed her the gardens, the barn, where we discovered the "treasures," and finally the house. Mom was working in the kitchen, preparing the pot roast for supper. Dad was reading the paper at the kitchen table. I introduced Mom and Dad.

"Would you like some iced tea, Iris? I just made it, so it might still be a little warm."

"That sounds lovely."

"Take your time. We'd better get back to help out. I can see the customer lull is over. When you're done, come look at our stuff. Maggie told me you can help yourself to veggies and flowers as our treat."

"Lovely. See you in a bit." She blew me another kiss. "That's some girl you've got, Emma."

"I know. We're very lucky." I smiled and blew both of the women kisses.

Eric and I walked back to the sale hand-in-hand. I kept thinking over and over again, like Dorothy, "There's no place like home."

CHAPTER 39

Stephen

August 1964

The sale officially ended at five, but since there were very few people still looking, we started to pack up fifteen minutes early and put everything on the front porch. However, there was one car left, a green and white Chevy late '50s, according to Eric, parked on the road with a man inside. He seemed unsure if he wanted to check things out.

Eventually, a tall, stoop-shouldered man got out of the car and walked in our direction. I could see that his face had been badly burned. He was wearing a hat to help hide his face and protect it from the sun. "Am I too late?"

"Never too late," I said. "Welcome. Look around." *Dollars to donuts that's Stephen Johnson.* "My name is Suze Bailey."

"Nice to meet you. Who's this young lady?" he asked when Carrie joined us, holding Berry.

"My name is Carrie and this is my cat Berry. Carrie and Berry. We rhyme."

"You certainly do. My name is Stephen. Pleased to

meet you."

"Stephen, what a pleasant surprise. I thought it might be you."

"You mean you already know Stephen?" Carrie gave me "the look."

"I do. He is Iris's nephew and he used to live here. I wrote to him inviting him to our sale."

"Groovy." Carrie hugged her cat and twirled around.

I grinned, but didn't laugh.

"Iris is in the house talking to Mom. Carrie, why don't you show Stephen around." *Let the interrogating begin.*

"Did you have chickens, pigs, and goats when you lived here? I don't count the cats and dogs 'cause everyone has those. Do you like gardens? We have a big one in back. Did you have a garden when you lived here?"

"Slow down, Carrie. Give Stephen a chance to answer your questions." I loaded up the wheelbarrow with whatever I could to take back to the porch. Fortunately, we sold quite a bit, so the take-down was much easier than the setup. I would also tell Iris her nephew was here.

When I went into the kitchen, Iris and Mom were chatting away like old friends.

"Iris is staying for supper."

"Great because I have a surprise for you, Iris. Stephen just showed up and Carrie is giving him the tour. You will finally be able to catch up."

Iris started to cry. "I haven't seen much of that boy since he was injured in the war. He got burned up pretty bad. I think he didn't want to startle people with his facial scars. When he did show up to family funerals, he tried to cover his face with a hat and never stayed to socialize. He moved to Red Wing after his parents died and pretty much became a recluse. This is unbelievable. Neither of us has much family left."

"Invite him to stay for supper. We've got plenty, especially with all the vegetables from the garden. Suze, please set another place at the dining room table."

"You betcha. Iris, you might want to rescue Stephen from Carrie."

Iris went to the back screen door and watched as Carrie, holding Stephen's hand, took Stephen into the barn. "I don't think he needs rescuing, Suze. He seems to be enjoying your sister immensely."

We noticed that when Stephen came in to wash up for supper, he had removed his hat.

* * *

After a delicious meal Stephen and Iris were about to go home when Carrie ran upstairs and came down with the stamps and the silver box with the coins to show Stephen.

"Look what I found in a cardboard box in the hay loft."

"Oh, I'd forgotten all about those," Stephen said as he opened the box and touched the coins. "My dad gave me those when I was a kid."

"Then they're yours. This, too." Carrie pulled a rumpled sheet of paper from her pocket. "It's ah ... ah an araisal?"

"An appraisal, sweetie," Maggie said.

"It means you're rich!" She gave Stephen a big hug.

"Yes, I am," Stephen said, looking at all of us. "Thanks

so much for the beautiful dinner. Iris will be staying with me in Red Wing tonight. We have lots to talk about." We loaded them up with veggies and flowers and said our good-byes.

"I love long Minnesota good-byes, don't you, Eric?"

"Ya, I sure do."

CHAPTER 40

A Short Good-bye

August 1964

Maggie took us to King's for lunch on our last day. We didn't keep our sale open very long on Sunday. Not much inventory left. I was feeling low-energy because of my cold, the letdown from the sale, and saying good-bye to the Rainbow House, Maggie, the animals, and most of all to Eric. For Eric and me the lunch was a rather somber affair. We enjoyed the 'burgers and fries, but not the prospect of saying good-bye.

Then Maggie and Nick surprised us, mid-lunch!

"Nick, I can't stand it any more. I have to tell them," Maggie said, grinning from ear to ear.

"What?" Carrie said with her mouth full. "I bet I know the secret. Maggie and Nicky sitting in a tree-ee..." Burger crumbs flew from her mouth.

"Shush, Carrie, let Maggie tell us and don't talk with your mouth full," Mom said.

"Nick and I are engaged to be married," Maggie blurted. Eric grinned. She showed us her left hand and sure enough she had an engagement ring: an emerald solitaire in a gold band. Simple, elegant, very Maggie.

"Eric, you knew and didn't tell me!" I gave him a friendly arm punch. I touched my locket from Eric, remembering how I'd almost lost it.

"It wasn't for me to tell," Eric said.

"When? Where? Come on, Sis, spill the beans."

"Can I get a new dress, a pretty one this time, not like that ugly yellow dress that looks like a mustard bottle. *EWW*."

"We have lots of things to figure out, including your dress, Carrie. Nick has to sell the house and we both have to get rid of some of the stuff we've accumulated. We're thinking of next June after Eric's graduation, probably mid to late June. We don't want to spoil Eric's day with wedding plans."

"Congrats, you two," Dad said after a big swig of beer. "Now we don't have to worry about you out here on your own."

"I think she's managed quite well 'on her own,'" Mom said. That woman was becoming quite the women's advocate. "I don't know how she's done it."

"Eric helped a lot. I couldn't have maintained my little farm without him. Now I get a two-for-one special. I'm such a lucky woman."

Okay, so Nick would be my step-uncle. I could handle that, but wouldn't that make Eric my step-cousin? Is it legal to date a step-cousin? I remember hearing that it was illegal in Minnesota to marry cousins. It was at Emily Miller's sleep-over when she said she liked her cousin. Then Kathy said, "*EWW. That's gross and against the law.*"

Come on, Girl. That was when there would be some weird genetic combinations from inbreeding, like mental illness. You are not genetically related, not related at all, except through marriage. Put that puppy to rest. You've got bigger problems like how do you keep a long distance relationship working? Hmm?

Okay, my inner bitch voice had a point. Where would Carrie and I stay when we'd visit? Would Eric get my old room? Could we see other people? Would he visit? Would I visit? Letters? Phone calls? My brain hurt just thinking about it. I needed to leave for a few minutes.

"Excuse me, I need to use the restroom."

"Me, too," Carrie said.

"No, honey, I think Suze needs to be alone. I'll check on her in awhile," Maggie said.

Maggie was kind enough to give me ten minutes or so of private time to get myself under control. I had so many questions about what their marriage would mean to me and Eric. I suppose that was selfish of me. I washed my face and was about to go back to our table when Maggie came in.

"Let's go for a little walk, across the street to the ballpark. We don't want to talk private stuff in King's ladies' room."

"Sure don't."

We heard a woman say, "Well, I never."

"Okay, so what's scaring you about my marriage to Nick?"

"I'm not scared exactly. I'm happy for both of you ... really. Nick's a great guy and you're great together, I'm just not sure what this means for Eric and me. It's kind of weird to be dating a guy whose dad is married to my aunt. I mean you'll be living in the Rainbow House together, so that means we'll be sharing a bathroom?"

"I see what you mean. I hadn't quite gotten around to thinking about logistics yet. Like where Eric will stay when you and Carrie visit. Having only one bathroom on the second floor does make things a bit awkward. It wouldn't bother Carrie, but I know how difficult that would be for you. Nick and I will talk about it. Anything else on your mind?"

"You mean other than leaving the Rainbow House, all the animals, and Eric? I got so used to seeing him every day. He was so easy to be around; we were so comfortable together. Everything is changing and I hate it!"

At that I burst into tears. Good thing we shared colds because I felt I could hug her without feeling like she would get infected.

"Well, I have two things that might cheer you up: a letter from Iris and some money from me." Maggie handed me one of her bluebird cards with a $100 dollar bill inside. I put Iris's letter in my pocket to read on the ride home.

"Maggie, it's too much."

"No, honey, it's not enough. I know how hard it will be on both of you, but Nick told me that he wants us all to visit St. Cloud in October to visit St. Cloud State. Eric is seriously thinking of going to school there. We can spend the day together and I promise we'll give you and Eric some private time."

"It won't be the same. Oh, Maggie, I'm going to miss it here."

"And we're going to miss you. I loved having you and Carrie with me for the summer. You okay?" I nodded. "Then let's join the others."

Eric and I said our good-byes in the King's parking

lot with lots of people around us. He shook hands with Dad, gave Mom, Maggie and Carrie hugs and finally said his good-bye to me. It was short, sweet, and sad.

We drove back to the Rainbow House, packed our clothes, and started to load the car. The plan was to take Berry back with us. Mom had bought a small cat carrier to transport her, but we couldn't find her anywhere. It was like she knew we were going to take her away from her home and hid to avoid leaving and saying good-bye. I knew just how she felt.

Poor Carrie was heartbroken. I suspect she was also coming down with "our" cold because she didn't throw her usual hissy fit.

"Honey, this is Berry's home. She loves it here. Maybe you need to let her stay with all her animal friends," Maggie said. "Eric, Nick, and I will take good care of her."

"But I'm her friend, too, and she's *my* friend. I found her and I took good care of her."

"You've been a good friend to her and given her excellent care. I tell you what. You go on home and we'll look for Berry. Maybe you can visit in a few weeks and take her home then. What do you say?"

"Okay, promise?"

"Promise."

"See, Suze, you had to leave Eric and I had to leave Berry. Now we can be sad together."

We got in the car, and waved good-bye to the Rainbow House and Maggie. Dad turned on the radio and we listened to the Twins on WCCO.

While Carrie slept, I read over Iris's letter and thought about my summer.

Dear Suze,

I don't know how I can properly thank you for reaching out to both me and Stephen. Please accept this small gift as a token of my appreciation. Buy yourself something new for school.

I had given up on Stephen out of respect for his need for privacy, but I can see now that was a mistake. There are so few of the Johnson clan left that we can't afford to be dismissive of those who remain. You reached out and connected us. For that, I will be forever grateful.

Stephen and I were comfortable with your family. He even removed his hat! You were all so gracious, warm, and welcoming (even the animals) that I would like, with your permission, to consider your family and my family "related" by house, the lovely Rainbow House.

And your little sister, what a character. Stephen was completely enamored with Carrie and her generosity. (So was I.) He had long forgotten about those "treasures" and if he ever does decide to sell them, he will greatly appreciate the "windfall."

We must remain in touch, Dear Friend.

Love,

Iris

CHAPTER 41

Gifts

Carrie, Eric, Maggie, Mom and I were all back in school. Eric and I exchanged weekly letters about our extracurricular activities, our friends, and our classes. We'd call each other if something extraordinary happened like if I bowled a 600 series (I did) or Eric got an "A" in a chemistry test (he did). I really missed him.

Mom was super busy, taking the "basic" classes at St. Cloud State. This quarter she had biology and psychology, which she was particularly enjoying because she could "analyze" her family at meals.

> *Mom: Sweetie, don't you think you should reevaluate this relationship with Eric? It's hard enough to maintain a healthy relationship when you see your "partner" on a regular basis. I think you're in "denial" about long term possiblilities.*

> *Me: Please pass the potatoes.*

Dad: Emma, don't forget our bowling league meeting on Monday night. Since I'm league president and you're league secretary, we've got lots to talk about.

Mom: Jake, you're so "anal" about our schedule. Lighten up. Connect with your "inner child." I've done the secretary bit forever. The "learning curve" is minimal.

Dad: Please pass the broccoli.

Carrie: I wanna show you what the teacher gave me at school today — (Carrie runs to her room mid-dinner and returns with a gerbil in her pocket.) I get to keep Pepsi for the weekend. Isn't he super cute? And look at those chibongas.

She sets Pepsi on the table where he nibbles the carrot on her plate.

Mom: Sweetie, we've really got to work on "impulse control." Now take the rodent and his chibongas back to his cage. Chibongas, *she's definitely "fixating." I wonder if she needs therapy.*

Dad: What's for dessert?

Mom's mealtime conversations seemed to focus on her ability to insert as many psych-vocab words as possible.

We were looking forward to second quarter when she'd be taking Art History and Freshman Communication.

Despite Mom's interest in psychology, she seemed much happier, less "controlling," less "obsessive" (Is psych vocab syndrome contagious?) about housework and easier to be around because she had a life and we were all better off. Dad especially. They both seemed much happier.

Carrie was her usual self — slightly obnoxious, snoopy, very talkative, but I had seen another side of Carrie this past summer. She actually thought of others once in awhile and didn't always have to get her way. Plus, Maggie taught the kid some responsibility, especially with Berry.

* * *

When I awoke the next morning, Mom and Dad were already awake.

"Kids, I've made pancakes and I've got a letter from Maggie." I don't know if it was the pancakes or the letter, but we both hightailed it to the kitchen.

"I wanna read it first," Carrie said, grabbing the envelope.

"Why don't you read it to us?" Mom said. "If you can't read Maggie's handwriting, I'll help."

Carrie ripped open the letter. "She printed it so that I could read it. Yay!"

Dear Suze and Carrie,

How are you adjusting to St. Cloud and school? You know me, the old teacher, wanting to check in with her "kids." I've been thinking of you both as I start this new school year.

I have twenty-six second graders who are wiggly little rippers; they remind me of a

*room full of puppies or kittens. Hmm, did
someone mention kittens?*

*You remember when Berry disappeared, how
disappointed you were, Carrie, that you
couldn't take her home with you. Well, she
was gone for over two weeks. When she
returned, she was hungry and beaten up so I
took her to the vet. He dressed her wounds,
gave her a series of vac-cin-a-tion —*

(Carrie sounded that one out.)

*— and a good once over. He sent me home
with antibiotics, some kitty vitamins, and a
hefty bill. But Berry's worth it. 'Cause . . .
guess who's going to be a mom? Not me, silly.
Berry!!!*

*Before you go nuts, Carrie, you need to know
the ges-ta-tion period —*

(Carrie stumbled over that word and Mom helped
with the pronunciation and definition)

*— for cats is fifty-seven to sixty-seven days,
so according to that, she will be delivering
kittens sometime mid-late November.*

*Because that's also Thanksgiving time, my
favorite holiday ever, I would like to invite
you and yours to have Thanksgiving dinner
and stay the weekend with me. Nick and Eric
will come and go, so no worries about sharing
the bathroom with Eric, Suze.*

(Carrie giggled when she read that.)

*I'm also inviting Stephen and Iris for
Thanksgiving dinner. Who knows? Maybe*

there will be kittens. I think you guys should pick out two. Yes, I said two. I said two because they will play with each other and not demand so much time and attention from your busy lives. I've had an only cat just once and she nearly destroyed the house. I suspect that might have been the real reason for the divorce. Just kidding.

You'll have to wait to take the kittens home until they're about seven to eight weeks old. They'll be Christmas or New Year's kitties.

Now talk this over with your mom and dad and see what they think of the plan. I'm excited for both of you. You'll each have a kitten of your own. Maybe Stephen would take one as well. A cat would make an excellent companion for him.

I can only hope that because it's her first litter, she'll have fewer babies. Who knew that a female as young as four months could get pregnant? If I'd known that, I would have had her spayed. Now I'll have to wait until the kittens are weaned.

Write back and tell me what your parents say. Relax, Emma, you'll love having two adorable fur balls batting your nose in the middle of the night and bringing you mousie gifts!

Have fun, but study hard.

Love you and miss you,

XXOO Maggie, Berry, Buddy Holly, Peggy Sue, Pickles, Mrs. Minniver, etc.

"We get two kitties! We get two kitties!" Carrie was beside herself, doing her pogo stick— jumping bean routine while singing the news.

"Enough already," Mom said. "I haven't agreed to Maggie's plan yet."

"Well, Berry was an outside kitty who had the run of the farm. She never would have been happy being confined to the house. We can raise these kittens to be house cats, so they'll be happy with us. I think it sounds like a fine plan," Dad said. *Way to go, Daddy-o!*

"Well, I guess that's that," Mom said. "It will be good for the girls to take responsibilty for the cats. And I did love my Willie."

"Still do," Dad said with a twinkle in his eye.

Chapter 42

Disappointment

October, 1964

I was so looking forward to Eric, Maggie, and Nick's visit. Boy, was I disappointed. They could only stay over one night because Eric had a school obligation on Saturday. I suspect it was his Homecoming Dance, but I didn't ask and he didn't volunteer any explanation. It was his senior year, after all, and I suppose he didn't want to miss the big semi-formal dance. I understood that, but it still hurt.

All those heart-to-heart talks we had over the summer and we never once discussed dating others; I just assumed we wouldn't because we promised to write and keep in touch. I felt so close and comfortable with Eric, but I now I believe this was just a summer romance, nothing more, at least for him.

You're living a song lyric, girl. Pathetic.

Maggie stayed with us, but Eric and Nick got a motel room. Most of Friday was spent touring the campus. I didn't mind that because I would probably end up at St. Cloud State as well. Mom and I could ride together. *Big whoop! Isn't that just every girl's dream? Not.*

It was fun to see the dorms, the student union and the main academic buildings. We had a "tour" guide from some fraternity; he talked mainly to Eric and we followed along like little kids on a field trip. I had very little private time with Eric, no holding hands, no hugs, no kisses. It was awkward and Maggie didn't help the situation. She and Mom were all about the wedding plans.

Maybe Eric and I would have time to talk over Thanksgiving. We were moving fast into the "just friends" lane. Plus, he was going to be in the family and I would be seeing him at all the family gatherings, so I had to get over it.

Bummer. C'mon, there are other "fish in the Mississippi." Nothing wrong with having a guy friend. And let's face it, for a first love, Eric wasn't bad, not bad at all. Lose a boyfriend. Gain a cat. A fair exchange. Sounds like it's time to move on, girlfriend.

Easier said than done. I hated it when my inner "bitch" voice was right.

That night I added the locket to my Memory Box.

CHAPTER 43

The Breakup

November 1964

"How are you feeling about seeing Eric again?" Mom asked as were packing for our long weekend at the Rainbow House.

"I finally got the nerve to ask him about Homecoming, and he told me he was going with a girl named Lisa, a senior. He didn't want to miss his last high school Homecoming dance. I get it. He said she was 'just a friend,' but they're still seeing each other. I was hoping we'd still be together, so in answer to your question, I'm not sure exactly how I feel. Maybe this family time will clear things up. I know how uncomfortable I felt when I last saw him. It was awkward, Mom, not at all like it was this summer."

"I know, honey. Long distance relationships, especially at your age, seldom work out. I'm sorry."

"Me too."

"It will all turn out okay. Trust your old mom. It is Thanksgiving, after all, and we should be grateful for our beautiful family, extended though it is."

"You're right. I'll try. It will really be good to see

everybody: Maggie, Nick, Iris and Stephen, all the animals, even Eric. What I'm really excited about are the kittens! What do you think — girls or boys or one of each?"

"I'm partial to the toms, provided they get neutered early. I wouldn't want them spraying the house, marking their territory."

"What do you think Carrie wants?"

"With her curiosity about chibongas, what do you think? Although he's not going to have them for long."

"Maybe one of each. Maggie says there are three females and two males. Each is marked differently and only one looks like Berry. I'll know when I see them which one I want."

"Berry probably mated with several toms, so each of the kittens could have a different father."

"Great, my kitten has a slut mom."

"Don't be so hard on Berry. When cats go into heat, any male will do."

"There are a few girls like that in my class," I said, laughing.

It was a perfect November morning: frosty, sunny, no wind to speak of. When we drove up the dirt driveway, I felt like I was coming home to the Rainbow House. I had missed it. All the Eric memories washed over me. My first love — Mom and Iris had warned me.

The colorful front porch was decorated with corn stalks, and pumpkins, lots of pumpkins. A few mums had survived the frost and provided some color. Maggie had made a wreath of grasses, grape vines, and bittersweet for the front door. We could smell the turkey from outside.

"Something smells nummy," Mom said. She was carrying the pies. Dad, Carrie, and I had the luggage. "I love Thanksgiving. No obligations, no gifts, just food. Lots and lots of food."

"Welome and Happy Turkey Day!" Maggie said. "Hugs all around."

"Where are the kittens?" Carrie said as she dropped the luggage in the hallway. "I get to pick first. Right, Maggie?"

"Take your stuff upstairs and I'll show you the kittens. They make the tiniest mews and their eyes are still closed, but you can get an idea of color and personality. There's one big ginger male who was the first born. He's almost twice the size of the others and a bit of a bully."

Maggie took us upstairs and showed us where Berry had nested. Wouldn't you know it — in *my* closet. Maggie had taken a large cardboard box and lined it with clean towels and old blankets, the same ones Carrie had used for the "privacy" box she made for Berry when we first found her. "The smell was familiar and she felt safe and secure in the box. She's been a very good mom."

We looked in the box and there they were, five little fur balls, nursing and kneading Berry's tummy. She was purring and quite content. Carrie was thrilled. "Can I pick them up?"

"Not quite yet. You should be able to by Saturday or Sunday."

"Berry, you are such a good mommy. I've missed you," Carrie said as she kissed her best friend's furry forehead. "Your babies are beautiful. Can I have one? I'll take very good care of him, I promise. I really like the one that looks like you."

"Let's leave Carrie to converse with the kitties,"

Maggie said. "I have something I want to show you." Maggie took me to her room and showed me the wedding dress she had made.

Made of a rich, creamy satin, the above-the-knee dress had cap sleeves, a scoop neck (a sweetheart neckline according to Maggie), and a fitted A line shape. Very simple, very elegant, very Maggie. "I'll be wearing flowers in my hair. That's it. Nothing fancy, nothing fussy. Just like I want my wedding to be. I thought I'd make your dresses, too. We just need to find a fabric and pattern you like. They don't have to match."

"When should we do this? The sooner the better I suppose."

"I'd like to get them done in the next three or four months, so that you can try them on. And then you can't lose or gain any weight. Understand?"

"Got it. But I don't have to watch my weight today. Bring on the turkey and all the trimmings."

"That's my girl. Speaking of turkey and trimmings, I'd better get back to the kitchen. The bird is calling. You can help peel the potatoes and set the table. I doubt we'll get Carrie away from the kittens."

"When are you expecting Nick, Eric, and the Johnsons?"

"I told them we'd eat at four. We'll have a good chat before they get here. I've missed you."

When we got to the kitchen, Mom was preparing the green bean casserole. Dad was in the living room watching football.

I was desperate to grill Maggie about Eric.

"Okay, Maggie, what's going on with Eric? We've written and talked a few times on the phone, but I'm not getting much info about this girl, Lisa. Are they dating or not? He says they're 'just friends.' What does that even mean? We were really good friends, too."

Maggie took a deep breath. "I think they are dating and I think they're more than 'friends.' He's worried that he's hurt you and is rather embarrassed about it. I know that it's hard to hear that he has another girlfriend, but that's the truth of the matter."

"I knew it deep down. Thanks for telling me. One more question then I'll let it go: Was he dating her while we were together this summer?"

"No, but they have known each other since grade school and only started dating after she asked him to the Homecoming dance."

"She asked him?" That made a difference. He didn't pursue her; she pursued him.

Does that really make a difference? He's got a mind of his own. He could have said, "No, I'm with someone." Instead he went to the Homecoming dance with Lisa. Get over it, so you can enjoy your dinner.

"Let it go, hon," Mom said.

"Does Iris know that we broke up? What if she says something? I just want this day to be over," I said, putting my head on the kitchen table.

"I get the kitty that looks like Berry," Carrie said, skipping into the kitchen. "When do we eat?" She took a look at the cranberry relish Maggie made and pronounced, "I'll name him Cranberry after his mother, Berry."

"I'm going to the barn to say hi to the animals."

"Can I . . .?"

"No, Carrie, not this time. I want to be alone."

I was greeting Buddy Holly, Peggy Sue and Pickles when I heard Eric say, "Suze, is that you? I thought you'd be inside helping with dinner."

"And I thought you wouldn't be arriving until three or three-thirty."

"I just wanted to do the chores a little early. You look good, Suze."

"You too. Well, I won't keep you from your chores." I started to leave and he caught me by my arm.

"Suze, I'm sorry. I never meant to hurt you."

"I know, but you did."

Eric hung his head.

"Since we'll be 'family' we need to move on, especially me. I wish you the best." I walked back to the kitchen to peel the potatoes.

CHAPTER 44

Surprise!

June 1965

"Here comes the bride, big, fat, and wide. And here comes the groo-oom skinny as a broom!" Carrie belted from the back seat of the car.

"Honey, you can sing that in the car, but not at the wedding. Understand?"

"How about *Crazy*? Nothing like a good Patsy Cline classic," I volunteered. Since Eric and I split, I was a little cynical about the whole wedding thing. Dad laughed. I did like my jade green satin sleeveless dress, though. Hoped it still fit.

"Tell me again why couldn't we take Cranberry and Munchkin with us?"

"They'd be terrified with all the changes to their lives, and Maggie has enough to worry about without our two kittens. The neighbors promised to check on them every day, feed them, clean the litter box. They'll be fine."

Mom, Dad, Carrie, and I got to the Rainbow House late on Friday afternoon. Mom brought sloppy joes and pasta salad, so Maggie wouldn't have to cook.

Nick and Eric were supposed to bring the beverages and dessert. Not exactly the traditional groom's dinner, but Maggie and Nick weren't exactly traditional.

I hadn't seen or communicated with Eric since Thanksgiving, and I had no idea what to expect. All the info I had, I got from Maggie. He was elected prom king, graduated with honors, planned to attend Winona State, gained weight, grew out his hair, blah, blah, blah. So when this bulked up, long-haired man rounded the corner carrying a pie I was totally blown away.

"Close your mouth, Suze, before the flies get in," Mom said with a grin. "Maggie warned you."

"Not about this!" I gestured in Eric's direction. What happened to my gangly, awkward, shy Eric? The guy who tried to fight Ace, the Red Wing bully, the guy who fell in the mud defending my honor, the guy who said "One Mississippi," the guy who stuck my bowling socks up his nose? Who was this guy anyway?

"Hey Suze, what's happenin'?" Eric sauntered up to me. He used to say, "Hey, Suze, what's the news?"

"Nothing much except a wedding," I said as I walked away. How could I have fallen for this guy? Even his dimples didn't impress me. He still had big ears, though they were camoflaged by his long hair, and big feet. No way to camouflage them. In a way, this was a good thing. My heart no longer fluttered, my tummy no longer flip-flopped. I had finally moved on. *Yay me.*

We ate our dinner, and then the guys got the big ladders from the barn and strung up white lights in the trees. While they were doing that, the "girls" arranged the picnic tables, donated by friends and neighbors, in the yard next to the garden. We would wait until tomorrow to add the red and white checked table cloths, candles and floral centerpieces.

When planning an outside June wedding, you have to have a contingency plan in case of rain, but Maggie and Nick were convinced they didn't need one because according to all sources, the weather would be beautiful. They listened to the news every day and watched the weather report every night and there was no, I mean no, indication that there would be rain. So when, on the morning of June 19th, there was still no rain in the forecast, we picked the flowers for Maggie's bouquet and the centerpieces and stored them in the barn where it was cooler. We would wait until the afternoon to actually "dress" the tables.

According to plan, the actual ceremony and reception were to be held in the backyard at four. Around two the clouds moved in, the sky darkened, and it poured.

"So much for having a contingency plan," Mom said to Maggie. "We could move the ceremony to the barn."

"What a romantic setting! The pigs, goat, and chickens as witnesses, I love it," Maggie said, laughing. I couldn't believe she was laughing.

"This is a disaster. Aren't you pissed-off?" I asked.

"There's nothing we can do about the weather, so why bother? I just want to get married. That will happen in the barn, on the porch, in the backyard, in the living room, regardless of weather."

"But what about the guests?"

"Are you kidding? These people are friends and family. They've been through a lot worse than a little rain. Besides this is a celebration."

"Maybe it will be over in an hour," Dad said. "We can only hope. Meanwhile, don't you ladies have to get ready?"

"Come on, girls, let's get beautiful."

"Here comes the bride, big, fat, and wide . . ." Carrie sang at the top of her lungs as we climbed the stairs. Maggie and I joined in.

"Carrie, I told you ... oh, what the hell," Mom said and joined us, only she changed the words:

"Here comes the bride, all dressed in pink. Open the windows and let out the stink." Carrie squealed in delight.

After an hour struggling to get hair, makeup and clothes just perfect, we heard a commotion from downstairs.

"Shit, how are we going to work in this kitchen? No counter space. Just keep piling food up on the table," the head caterer said to his lackeys. "And it had to start raining. Where are we going to set up the buffet?"

"Sounds like the caterers," Maggie said. "This will be a challenge, considering the weather. We might have to set up the buffet in the dining room."

That's exactly what happened.

Maggie had asked Mrs. Wiederholdt to cater the wedding. She accepted on one condition: Maggie had to supply the supper club with produce and flowers for the next two months. Wiederholdt's provided the dishes, glassware, napkins and the food, of course. Nick was providing the bubbly, the only alcohol being served, and that would be served with Maggie's gooey, chocolate layer cakes.

The wedding menu consisted of Wiederholdt's signature items: barbequed ribs and chicken, baked potatoes with all the fixins, homemade rolls, a large garden salad with homemade dressings. Beverages, served outside, included iced tea, soft drinks, and coffee with Nick's bubbly to go with the cake.

The forty guests lined up on the front porch, got their food and went out the kitchen back door to the picnic tables once the rained stopped. Most of the guests had been to Maggie's before the wedding, so there was less need to try to impress.

Good thing too, since the kitchen looked like a war zone. Maggie wasn't that kind of girl anyway. What you saw was what you got. This was a picnic celebration at a farm, after all, and it was supposed to be relaxed and fun! And it was a blast.

Maggie's school buddies had set up a record player and speakers in the barn and provided a steady stream of appropriate music, from Big Band '40s stuff, to Elvis and the Beatles. There was no dance floor, but people managed a few slow dances on the grass. Mostly there was friendly conversation, laughter, and good will all around.

The guests started to drift away around nine. By this time, the caterers had cleared away the food, stored the leftovers in the refrigerator, packed up the dishes, and cleaned the kitchen.

Maggie and Nick left around ten for Red Wing to stay the night in a little B&B. Eric had left much earlier. I suppose I should have told Maggie that he could bring Lisa, but I just couldn't do it. I had moved on, but not that much. It was better that he left early, before the romantic music was played, because I might have done something stupid after a glass or two of bubbly.

Dad was in the barn, making sure all the animals were settled. Mom had started gathering table cloths. The neighbors would be picking up their picnic tables tomorrow. Carrie was putting the candles in a box, and I was making a mess of the flower centerpieces.

"Why don't we wait until tomorrow for the flowers? Maybe the neighbors could each take a centerpiece when they pick up their tables," Mom suggested.

"Good idea. I'm too tired to deal with them. Man, weddings are a lot of work."

"Nothing compared to marriage," Mom said.

"I'm beginning to understand that," I said, thinking back to last summer. "Have I ever told you how much I love and appreciate you and Dad? You're the best."

Chapter 45

News from Suze

September, 1965

Dear Maggie,

I thought you might get a charge out of this essay, the first of the year, on the topic of "Most Significant Summer Event," a variation of "How I Spent My Summer Vacation."

Why can't English teachers come up with something more original? I had a blast writing it (I'm guilty of some exaggeration.) and I hope you'll have fun reading it. By the way, I got an "A."

Love,

Suze

"News from Suze"

by Susan Bailey

Live from Miesville, home of the

Mudhens and King's Bar and Grill, "News from Suze," brought to you by Wiederstuff's Supper Club. Heeeeere's — Suze!

Welcome to the social event of the summer: the wedding of renowned poet, gardener, teacher and artist, Maggie Thomas, and Cannon Falls' own Good Samaritan, Red Wing business man, and all around good guy, Nick Watson.

It's June 19th at the Rainbow House, the multicolored 100-year-old farmhouse, owned by the bride. Imagine an expansive, lush lawn with extensive perennial gardens and a breathtaking backyard garden as the setting for this idyllic and rustic celebration. Imagine trees decorated with white fairy lights and tables set with red and white checked tablecloths, candles and colorful floral centerpieces.

Imagine blue skies, sunshine, moderate temps, and low humidity, exactly what the forecasters predicted. And then wham! Surprise. The skies darkened, the wind gusted and the rain pelted sprayed hairdos and table centerpieces, the sounds of thunder drowned out the music, and lightning competed with the fairy lights. With ruined hairdos, wet clothes, and muddy shoes, the guests ran into the barn where all the snug, smug, and dry animals were waiting to witness the ceremony.

Pigs, chickens, and yes, even the goat watched as Maggie made her soggy entrance. Now for all you fashionistas out there, here is a fashion rundown, the way the "girls" looked pre-deluge:

Carrie Elizabeth Bailey, niece of the bride and flower girl: Ms. Bailey, with her dream of finally being a "Princess," chose a pink, green, and lavender print, puffy sleeved, long dress that just covered her Mary Janes.

"I'm finally a princess," she said as she twirled in circles. "And I love my hair up and curly. Don't you? Now can I throw flowers? That damn goat better not eat 'em."

Suzan Marie Bailey, niece of the bride and bridesmaid: Her curvaceous body, covered in a sleeveless, above-the-knee, jade green satin sheath, caused the best man, Eric Ray Watson, to gasp at her beauty. Even the animals were stunned into silence, except for Mrs. Miniver, the alpha chicken, who continued to cluck.

Ms. Bailey's naturally curly dark brown hair sexily escaped her French twist ala Audrey Hepburn.

When the poor groomsman saw that, he almost needed resuscitation. Oh, yes, she was carrying a multicolored floral bouquet designed and prepared by the bride. Sorry, I got carried away watching the sexually charged glances between the best man and bridesmaid.

Emma Bailey, sister of the bride and matron of honor: Wearing a satin-lined white lace sleeveless top over fitted black pants with slightly flared legs, her longer hair in a fashionable Jackie Kennedy flip, she looked stunning. The ensemble was completed by black satin low-heeled pumps and a bouquet of colorful flowers from Ms. Thomas's award winning garden.

Maggie Thomas, bride, and star of the show: Designed and created by the bride, the creamy satin A-line with cap sleeves and a sweetheart neckline was perfect. She had assessorized with pearl drop earrings, a gift from the matron of honor, and a simple floral crown that she made that morning with daisies and baby's breath, the same flowers used in her bridal bouquet.

The bride was perfectly composed as she walked to meet the groom in front of the pigs' pen.

"Dearly Beloved, blah, blah, blah, you may kiss the bride." And boy, did he!

Just as the kiss ended, so did the rain. As the bride, groom, and attendants exited the barn, along with their soggy guests, the sun came out. The crowd applauded and cheered as Maggie threw her bouquet.

Unfortunately, it landed in the mud and no one wanted to pick it up, considering this was a farm and all.

"Maggie, look a rainbow!" Carrie, the adorable flower girl, squealed with delight. "A rainbow at the Rainbow House!"

A perfect ending for the perfect wedding.

This is a slightly damp Suze with the News signing off live, from Miesville, Minnesota, home of the Mudhens, King's Bar and Gill and Wiederstuff's Supper Club.

* * *

Suze,

This is a delightful interpretation of the assignment. You've done a fabulous job setting the scene and describing the chaos and joy of the day. Even though you haven't directly addressed why this event was significant to you, through your writing, I understood how important your family is and how much you love them. Now that was significant enough for me.

Plus, you made me laugh. As a teacher reading so many of these, that was a real treat. Excellent work — A

Dear Suze.

Without a doubt, your essay was the best wedding gift ever.

XXOO

Maggie

CHAPTER 46

Looking Back

September, 2018

Nineteen sixty-four was a tumultuous year. Johnson signed the Civil Rights Act, race riots ensued, the Gulf of Tonkin Resolution gave Johnson authorization to use force in Vietnam, the Warren Commission investigated the Kennedy assassination, Martin Luther King Jr. received the Nobel Peace Prize, the first Ford Mustang was manufactured, women were still stuck in the '50s, but getting restless, the Beatles took the country by storm. None of that mattered at the Rainbow House, except maybe the Beatles and the occasional "restless" woman.

That summer we lived in a world without the gadgets and gizmos of modern technology. When we wanted to have a private phone conversation, we stretched the phone cord to talk in the closet. We enjoyed being outdoors every day because we gardened, cared for the animals, had our veggie stand and didn't have air-conditioning.

We read and listened to the radio because Maggie's TV was always on the fritz. We'd never even eaten a frozen pizza before that summer. Can you imagine? We conversed at the kitchen table every meal. We connected.

Maggie needed us that summer and boy, did we need her.

I remember feeling happy and secure, even though our parents struggled, because I was living in a bubble of innocence where violence was limited to a shouting match between Eric and a Red Wing bully after a baseball game and war was limited to memories and letters.

I saw what war could do when I met Stephen and when I talked to my mother about her first love who was killed in N. Africa. I couldn't possibly imagine losing friends to the Vietnam war, but I did. Over 1,000 Minnesotans were killed in Vietnam, including Ace from Red Wing. But I didn't know that when I was seventeen and living with Maggie in the Rainbow House.

As we all grew older and the outside world penetrated our "bubble," we changed and grew.

Mom went on to graduate from St. Cloud State with an art major. She ended up teaching at my old high school. Poor Carrie had to deal with having an attractive, talented Mom on the faculty. Not easy for the girl. Mom showed her sculptures in various art shows and galleries, but she never again attempted to carve another vegetable, thank God.

She and Dad continued working at their marriage and remained relatively happy. They stayed in their home near the hospital until Mom got dementia in her early seventies. Dad would find her wandering the neighborhood, confused and scared.

Out of necessity, they moved into an assisted living

facility. Once they left the family home, Mom's feisty spirit was gone, along with her will to live. Soon she stopped walking and eating. She died in 1994. Dad followed in 1998.

Carrie escaped St. Cloud by going to the University of Minnesota and majoring in biology and chemistry. Because of her excellent GPA, test scores, and favorable letters of recommendation, she was admitted to the U's Vet school and graduated with her DVM in 1982.

Miss "I can do it myself" and "You aren't the boss of me" never married, though she had several long-term relationships. Carrie and Stephen stayed in touch throughout the years and when he died, he bequeathed to Carrie the sterling silver box, the coins, the stamp collection and the appraisal that she once gave him.

Iris told me that Carrie "saved" Stephen from total isolation. That's why when Iris died, she passed on a sizable inheritance to Carrie which she donated to the local Wildlife Rehab Center where she regularly volunteered.

Carrie once told me that she liked animals more than she liked people. "Animals don't betray you, lie, cheat, or bully. They aren't ruled by monetary greed." Wherever she'd lived, she'd always had cats as beloved companions, none more dear than her first rescued cat, Berry. We have had times when we've been close and times when we've been distant, but we've always been sisters.

Maggie and Nick stayed in the Rainbow House for their entire marriage. She continued to teach, write, and create culinary surprises well into her sixties. Even after many years of marriage, she insisted we "girls" make pickles together each August when she harvested the cukes. Maggie stopped selling veggies once she got sick in January 2001. The cancer quickly spread and she succumbed August 20th, 2001 with Nick, Carrie, and me by her side.

Carrie was the "pray-er" and officiated at the funeral ceremony which was held in the Rainbow House backyard. Unlike the wedding, the sun shone and the sky was blue. The mourners were dry. The rainbows were in our hearts. Nick was never the same after her death. Neither were we.

Eventually Nick moved to California to be close to Eric, his wife, and grandchildren. After he moved, he made sure that Maggie's beloved Rainbow House stayed with Carrie and me as per Maggie's request. Carrie didn't want the responsibily of taking care of such a large property, so Gary and I bought her out. At first she refused payment, but then re-considered and donated most of it to the local Humane Society.

My husband, Gary, and I moved into the Rainbow House in 2005. We kept the house the same, as much as possible anyway. My bluebird room and Carrie's garden room stayed exactly the same. However, we did remodel the kitchen, but painted the walls the same lipstick red Maggie adored.

Iris, Carrie's benefactor, turned out to be mine as well. It was Iris who gave me the money to go to Macalester in St. Paul on the condition that I become a history major and visit her regularly. Not a hard sell at all.

It was at Macalester that I met Gary, an awkward, shy, intelligent, funny guy who shared my love of history. We met at a party and hit it off right away. I generally hated parties and so did he, so we left and talked. We ended up talking for the next two years. It wasn't until my first year of teaching that I realized that I loved my best friend. Two years later we married, and Maggie and Nick hosted our reception at the Rainbow House. "I was hoping you and Eric would, you know," Maggie said. "But I really like Gary. I'm so happy for both of you." I remembered what Mom and Iris said about first loves and how they stayed with you forever. Eric had become a sweet memory of my first, not my only, love.

Like Maggie and Mom, I became a teacher. Gary and I settled in St. Paul, close to the high school where I was teaching and close to Iris. We hoped to become parents, but, for whatever reason, I never conceived.

Then in 1977 we adopted a year-old, malnourished infant girl from Korea. We named our daughter Emma after Mom. She grew into a fine young woman, a teacher like her mom, aunt, and grandmother. Each year in August I buy pickling cukes at the Farmer's Market in Hastings and Emma and her girls join me for canning Maggie's award winning garlic dills.

Most of my thirty-five year career was spent with high school kids and I approached teaching history by connecting it as much as possible with personal experience. The approach worked, for the most part. I shared Wouk's *Winds of War* with the kids; some even chose to read it.

I told them about Matthew, Mom's first love who was killed in Africa, and about Stephen who came back disfigured and emotionally scarred. Soon they were sharing their own stories and bringing family artifacts and treasures from other wars. And it wasn't just about war. I brought in Maggie's quilts and we talked about quilting as a part of Civil War history, the Westward movement, and the history of women.

For her final project, one student made a quilt of historical events that personally impacted her life. I like to think I got kids to think about history as a living, breathing, ever changing force that could teach us if we were willing to learn.

"It's a beautiful evening, Suze, let's take the dogs for a walk," Gary said after Emma, her husband, and the kids had left for St. Paul. We walked hand in hand up the driveway and back, then on the path behind the barn toward the dump where we found so many "treasures."

Back in the garden, Gary and I sat on the picnic table, watching the sunset, when we heard a commotion in the trees. There perched throughout the trees was a flock of twenty or thirty bluebirds, the color of the summer sky on their backs, the color of rusty metal on their breasts. I'd never seen that many at one time.

Then I remembered Carrie's sweet little girl voice as she sang, "Somewhere over the rainbow, bluebirds fly" and her belief that bluebirds were a sign of happiness.

She was right.

The End

"The thought of our past years in me doth breed/Perpetual benediction..."

— *Wordsworth's* Ode

ABOUT BARBARA GRENGS

Barbara Grengs is a retired English teacher who reads, writes, gardens, and knits. She currently resides in Roseville, Minnesota with her one dog.

Acknowledgements

As always, I'm grateful for my early readers: Lee Johnson, Susan Holthaus, Joyce Hebert, Mary Peterson, and Laurel O'Gorman. They've provided keen eyes, generous hearts, support and encouragement.

Thanks to Judith Bergerson, my dear friend and extraordinary artist, who has designed the covers for all my books. She manages to distill the book into a beautiful work of art.

To Suzan St. Maur, who has written favorable reviews along the way, I appreciate your kind words and witty commentary.

To Arline Chase, my publisher and stalwart promoter, I'm forever grateful you took a chance on an "old" English teacher. Thanks for coming out of retirement and doing one more "for the road."

To my dear partner, Lee Johnson, my biggest fan since high school, thanks for suggesting the T.S. Eliot and Wordsworth quotes. Most of all, thanks for believing in me.

And finally to my daughter, Carrie, for the use of her name and her cheeky personality. Love you, sweetie.

Books by Barbara Grengs

Books for Grown-ups

Delicate Dames

Books for 16 years and Up

Rainbow House

Books for Grades 5 and Up

The Toby Martin Series

Toby Martin Pet Detective
Toby Martin School Sleuth
Toby Martin In-House Investigator
Toby Martin Park Patrol
Toby Martiin State Fair Security
Toby Martin Private Investigator

37156161R00158

Made in the USA
Middletown, DE
22 February 2019